THE
RETURNERS

THE
RETURNERS

GEMMA MALLEY

BLOOMSBURY

LONDON BERLIN NEW YORK

Bloomsbury Publishing, London, Berlin and New York

First published in Great Britain in February 2010 by Bloomsbury Publishing Plc
36 Soho Square, London, W1D 3QY

A CIP catalogue record of this book is available from the British Library

All papers used by Bloomsbury Publishing are natural,
recyclable products made from wood grown in well-managed forests.
The manufacturing processes conform to the environmental
regulations of the country of origin.

Typeset by Dorchester Typesetting
Printed in Great Britain by Clays Ltd, St Ives Plc, Bungay, Suffolk

Hardback ISBN 978 1 4088 0091 1

1 3 5 7 9 10 8 6 4 2

Paperback ISBN 978 1 4088 0090 4

1 3 5 7 9 10 8 6 4 2

www.bloomsbury.com

For Atticus and Allegra

PROLOGUE

There was this day, a few weeks ago. I was walking by the river, like I do sometimes, and maybe I was tired, or maybe I just felt like sitting down, I don't know – it doesn't matter. The point is, I sat down on one of those benches that have people's names on them, dead people, dead people who used to sit there before you did, maybe before you were even alive. I was just sitting there, hanging out. I wasn't doing anything in particular. Wasn't thinking about anything in particular. Watching the ducks, mostly, as far as I can remember. I saw a few people I know – Claire, Yan, walking along, maybe holding hands. I wasn't looking; it's nothing to do with me whether they were holding hands or not. I couldn't care in the slightest – but I pretty much ignored them like I usually do. Other people are overrated in my opinion. Unlike ducks. I mean, how could a duck ever upset you? Ducks don't look at you like you're a total freak, or say stupid things, or ask you questions they know you don't want to answer. Ducks just hang out, like I was doing. They just get on with it.

The reason I'm telling you this is that, as far as I can remember, that day was the last time I felt happy. That is the last thing I can remember before everything changed.

Stupid thing is, I didn't even feel particularly happy at the time. But you don't, do you? I mean, you don't generally wake up and think, 'You know what? I'm really happy today.' It's afterwards that you realise – when you look back. Happiness is weird like that. It's not like the pictures you see in adverts of people grinning manically, throwing children in the air and whooping just because they've bought some crappy washing powder or something. That kind of happiness doesn't exist. At least, I've never felt that way. Happiness – well, it's more like a photograph of someone you keep somewhere safe to look at every so often. You look at it and you feel warm and sad because the person's gone and you realise that when they were there the sun seemed to shine more. It's kind of screwed up – like happiness never just 'is'; it always 'was'. Or maybe that's just me.

Anyway, I didn't know that was going to be the beginning. I didn't know who I was back then. *What* I was. Back then, I could hang out by the river watching the ducks for hours and it didn't matter. Back then, I was just Will Hodges. Hodge, or Will, depending on whether I knew you, liked you. Most people call me Hodge. Which suits me – less personal. Hodge was just someone sitting at the back of the class, walking nonchalantly down the corridor. No one worried much about Hodge, which was just as I liked it. I could take care of myself. Hodge was a survivor.

Mum used to call me Will.

A very long time ago.

But that's not important. What is important, what I want you to remember, is that you never know. You never know when everything is going to change, when everything you've taken for granted for years and years is going to get smashed to pieces and you'll realise that there's nothing you can do, there's no way out.

Or maybe there is. But you've got to find it. And even if you do find it, that's never the end. It's only ever just the beginning.

CHAPTER ONE

I like it here. It's probably one of my favourite places. Don't know why. Or maybe I do. There's something about the river at dusk. In the spring, I mean. When the sky goes all red and pink and there's no one around – and even if there is, they don't stay for long, rushing away to whatever it is they've got to do. What's so important anyway? I bet if people thought about it for a moment they'd realise that all the rushing is a complete waste of time. Chill out, I say. Forget about it. Like the ducks.

Ducks are cool. Whatever happens, whatever gets thrown at them, they just carry on, their little legs paddling. Unfazed. They always look like they're smiling.

I found her here, when she died. Mum, I mean. I can remember bits about that day, but then I think maybe I'm just remembering the stories I've been told, because I remember different things at different times, things that don't really add up, like a series of photographs but the continuity is all wrong.

I didn't talk about it at all, apparently. Didn't even go for help – I guess I knew it was too late for that – I just sat there watching, watching over her. She was floating, face up, her long hair splayed out over the water like a painting. She was peaceful. Not like in real life, not in the months before. She'd be happy one minute and crying the next, and I could never see why. I was eight when she did it. Threw herself into the river to escape it all, to escape from her life, from me. They said I shouldn't take it personally; they said it was nothing to do with me. But I knew even then they were wrong. Mums generally don't throw themselves in rivers. Not when things are going OK.

I knew immediately it was my fault. Afterwards I remember my heart clenching slightly every time Dad left the house, in case he was going to go off too.

He didn't, though. He's still around.

She was nice, my mum. When she wasn't laughing and playing, or locking herself in the bathroom in tears, she used to sew things, knit things. I had a million jumpers, all in weird colours and sometimes a mad mix of clashing hues because she'd found some wool on sale, because they'd caught her imagination. She had a lot of imagination, my mum. She used to tell me stories about witches and wizards and ghosts and ghouls, but never really scary ones. She talked like the witches and ghosts were on our side; it was

5

the humans you had to watch out for, the humans who'd betray you and let you down.

The only other humans in our house were me and Dad. I guess we let her down quite a lot really. We didn't mean to. He works hard, my dad. He doesn't always have time. And I could have worked harder, could have helped more.

Could have. What a pointless couple of words.

They used to tease me at school about the jumpers. But the funny thing – funny in retrospect, I mean – was I always defended them. Vociferously, like my life depended on it, like those jumpers were more important than anything else in the whole wide world. Maybe they were. Maybe I knew deep down how easily they'd unravel if you just picked at one for a bit. Like Mum. I don't even know why I was down by the river. I mean, I'm eight, and I find her? Like, I'm on my own? The river's a good ten minutes' walk from our house.

So it doesn't make sense. She wouldn't have taken me with her. You don't kill yourself in front of your eight-year-old son.

Then again, she was sick, wasn't she? I mean, that's what they told me.

I'd ask Dad but ... Actually, I wouldn't ask Dad, not even if you paid me. We don't mention Mum in our house. Well, he does from time to time but only when he's really irritated about something, usually me, and then it's just to blame her. You're just like her, he'll say. God, you inherited your brain from your mother. You know you'll end up like her if you carry on like that, don't you?

That used to make me angry, really angry, like a white fire that started in my belly and shot out to my head, my hands, my legs, all of which would lash out uncontrollably. That's what Mum was scared of. The white anger. Dad has it too – you know when you've gone too far, when you've said something to make him really angry, because his eyes change. They go kind of flat and dull and you know you're in for it then. We're the same in that way. I don't let it take hold any more, though. I control it, bury it, push it somewhere, anywhere. You can't go succumbing to anger, or any other emotion for that matter. You just have to get on with it. If someone upsets you, just pretend they don't exist. That's what I do anyway. Life's much easier that way.

Her hair was long. Really long. No one else's mum had hair like hers. I used to tell her sometimes that it was too long, but she wouldn't get defensive or angry like Dad would if I told him something about the other dads at school, about their cars or their jobs or their appearance at sports day. She'd just smile serenely and say that one day she'd grow it right down to the ground, and I'd tell her that was impossible and she'd wink and say nothing was impossible. That's what she was like on good days – bubbly, funny, magic. And on bad days, it wasn't her fault, she was just taken over by something. Depression, Dad called it. I figured it was a bit like the white rage that Dad and I shared, but worse because it lingered, sucking every bit of happiness out of her, leaving her listless, unaware of anything or anyone around her. She used to just sit there and rock back and forward and even if I threw myself at her she didn't bat an eyelid, just kept right on going.

For ages I wondered if I'd done something to upset her. I don't wonder about it any more. I mean, you can't spend your life looking for answers to questions you're never going to get, can you? OK, maybe you can, but then you end up like Mum, rocking back and forth like a loon.

I didn't mean that. She wasn't a loon. She was nothing like a loon. If someone else had said that, I'd have them on the floor now, kicking them in the head and making them take it back.

No, I wouldn't. But I'd be mad as hell.

I must have told someone at some point. Or maybe someone saw me and thought it was a bit weird that an eight-year-old kid was standing by the side of the river, staring into it. I think sometimes I remember Dad being there, remember him talking to me, holding me really tight then walking away. But that doesn't make any sense, not really. What I'm sure I do remember is the people. Lots of them all crowding around me, asking me questions, touching me, trying to move me. Someone shouting that she'd been killed by 'one of them', that there would be vengeance for her death; a policeman telling him, 'It was suicide, mate.' Suicide. Did I know what the word meant? Of course I did. Even if no one had ever told me, I knew. I remember trying to ignore them, wishing that they'd go away, putting my hands over my ears like if I couldn't hear them then they weren't really there.

And I remember the other ones too. The ones who didn't say anything, the ones I'd felt around me before but never acknowledged. The freaks. I knew even then they were different. They were with the others in the crowd but separate somehow. They looked at me mournfully, like they knew, like they knew everything. But how could they? How could anyone know? I still don't know now, still haven't got a clue.

I asked Dad once about the freaks I saw there. He just raised an eyebrow, like it was a really dumb question. 'You think someone throwing themselves into the river doesn't attract attention? You don't think there were policemen and ambulancemen and nosy passers-by? Of course there were bloody people there. Think, will you, Will, before you ask unnecessary questions.'

Dad doesn't like unnecessary anything. He's a lawyer who works for the government, prosecuting criminals and making sure justice is done. Which means he's always sifting through papers and evidence to compile his cases. Outside work he likes things concise and to the point, nothing extraneous, nothing that isn't absolutely essential.

Mum dying was hard on Dad too. He got shorter.

His hair went grey really quickly. We never talked about it, but I heard him sob himself to sleep, heard him shouting at the television in a rage. Claire said he was the one who needed to talk to someone, not me. But no one was going to tell him that to his face – especially not me.

Claire's my neighbour. Not my next door one, but my bottom of the garden one. We used to be good friends. I used to hang out at her house a lot. You can see her window from mine – her garden backs on to ours – and I used to climb over the fence sometimes, late at night when Dad thought I was asleep, and shin up to her window. We'd sit in her room talking, playing video games, watching films. She had a television in her room. I don't know if she does now. We don't really see each other any more. Only in school and I don't like to spend any more time than is absolutely necessary *there*.

Her parents were funny. Are funny. Not in a ha-ha way, more in a weird way. I used to really like them. Now I don't know. They're probably all right. Dad says they're dangerous liberals. It's probably because they let Claire watch television whenever she wants to. He always thought Mum spent too much time with them. I asked him why, once, but he looked like he was going to hit me so I didn't wait around for an answer.

They don't watch television themselves, Claire's mum and dad, which is pretty weird when you think about it. They sit around talking and reading stuff to each other, like articles from the *Guardian*. They play board games. And they're always asking questions. You can never just sit there zoning out – it's always so, Will, how's school going? Are you enjoying Maths this year because you were finding it a bit difficult last year, weren't you? Is that a new bicycle, Will? Are you still playing tennis, Will? How's your Dad getting on, Will? Does he have any interesting cases on at the moment? It's relentless.

Was relentless. Like I said, I haven't been there in a while.

Dad, on the other hand, doesn't go in for questions. We don't talk about our stuff; we just get on with it and say what has to be said. Pass the tomato ketchup. We need some milk. The school called again – if I find out you've missed one more class I'm going to give you a hiding you'll remember till Christmas . . .

He used to talk more. When Mum was alive. He used to tell us about his cases. Tell us about the clever arguments he employed, about the ways he tripped up witnesses. I used to think he was so great, protecting the innocent, making things OK after bad things happened.

Turns out no one can do that. Turns out bad things happen and there's nothing you can do about it.

The area that we live in, it's what's known as a leafy commuter-belt town. Which basically means it's over-priced, there's nothing to do and we're expected to feel lucky all the time because there aren't gangs rampaging through our streets, or people being knifed, or drugs being sold on every street corner. All Dad's money gets swallowed up in the mortgage; it's a sacrifice he's made for me. He doesn't actually say it; I just feel it every time I ask him for money. Felt it, rather. I don't ask him for money any more. We used to have more money. He used to be a defence lawyer in a big law firm. He had a big car and wore smart suits and crisp white shirts, and Mum used to shop in Marks and Spencer.

But then the recession came and everyone started losing their jobs. Dad lost his in 2009. I remember the day – I got back from school and he was sitting on the sofa, staring at the wall, and when I asked him what the matter was, he just looked at me blankly and shrugged, not in an I-don't-know way but in an isn't-it-obvious way. Mum ushered me away, and told me that there wasn't enough work for him at his firm, that he'd been 'let go'. Which I didn't like the sound of because it sounded scary, like a balloon that's come out of your hand and is floating down the street and you just know it's going to bump against something hard and sharp and get popped. And Dad shouted out that 'There *was* enough work. They'd found work for *him*. If they think holding on to foreigners and letting Brits go is how to claw the way out of recession, then they deserve to go bankrupt', but Mum ignored him and gave me a kiss and told me it was time for tea.

For a few weeks Dad didn't get out of his dressing

gown at all, not even to go down the road to get a newspaper. I started taking a packed lunch into school. And Mum didn't go out with her friends any more with her dangly earrings and louder voice than normal when she got home.

He got another job, though, eventually, working for the Crown Prosecution Service. Now he's the one who prosecutes criminals instead of defending them. His friend Patrick helped. Mum didn't like Patrick, but Dad always told her that Patrick was one of the good ones, a patriot, that he wasn't going to let the country sink into the shit like everyone else. He started talking like Patrick too, calling the people he prosecuted 'thugs' and 'wasters', even though Mum said they hadn't been proven guilty yet.

There aren't that many thugs and wasters around here, but what we do have in this leafy commuter-belt town are off-licences where people hang outside waiting for someone's older brother or someone else they recognise who might do them a favour and buy them a bottle of something. We also have Parents' Drinks Cabinets, which they probably don't have in inner-city estates – Claire's parents, for example, have a huge cabinet dedicated entirely to the storage of booze, along with a wine cellar that is full of the stuff. Other than that, there's an arcade in the high street full of bored people playing boring video games, a shopping mall where all the girls seem to hang out, mostly giggling at nothing as far as I can tell, and a café where you can get a Coke for 50p and sneak a fag from the woman behind the counter for another fifty.

In spite of the wide variety of alcoholic beverages on offer, I don't drink. I've got enough problems without turning into a drunken idiot like the ones you see stumbling out of the pub in the middle of the afternoon.

They sent me to a shrink a few months after Mum died. I think the school had something to do with it, or maybe the doctor, I don't know. Dad didn't want me to go, said shrinks put stupid ideas in your head, made you think about things best left alone, but they said I had to go anyway. The shrink said he thought I was paranoid. Dad told me that was another word for mad, said I needed to pull myself together, to move on, to just get on with it. He said I had to sort it out because if I didn't . . . He didn't finish that sentence but we both knew what he meant. He meant I'd end up in the river like Mum.

The shrink pretended he didn't think I was mad. He kept asking about the freaks, only I could tell from his voice that he didn't believe a word I said. Didn't believe that they follow me, that they're always there, that there are more of them all the time. He made a big deal about them turning up just after Mum died, like I invented them to keep me company or something. I mean, the man was an idiot. If I was going to invent people to keep me company, they'd be nothing like the freaks. Nothing at all, trust me.

*   *   *

14

It started with one or two. It happens, doesn't it? You're walking down the street or something and you see someone you think you recognise, and they look like they recognise you too, right? Only when you get nearer you realise you don't know them. Or at least you can't place them. And so you walk past them. It's happened to us all, right?

Well, it happens to me all the time. Sometimes I think that every other person is looking at me, staring at me, that they know me, that they know something about me. The shrink thought I was delusional, I realised. He was probably right too. You can't be completely sane if you see eyes staring at you all the time, haunted, sad-looking eyes boring into you, eyes that you recognise, that recognise you; except you don't really recognise them because you don't know them, you know you don't – you've been through every person you've ever met in your life and they are none of them . . . You don't have that unless you're loop the loop.

That's probably why Claire and I don't see each other any more. She probably thinks *I'm* a freak.

I don't blame her. Sometimes *I* think I'm a freak too.

CHAPTER TWO

I'm on my way home from the river, but I've got something in my shoe. A stone. Small one. I can't be bothered to get rid of it – untying the laces, standing on one leg. The stone could have got into my sock. I'm not taking that off too. I'm on my way home anyway. It'll be fine. I thrust my hands in my pockets. It doesn't matter. It's just a stone.

I see Claire on the other side of the river, without Yan this time. I'm pleased about that. Don't know why, really. It's no skin off my nose who she hangs out with. I don't wave. Why would I? She hasn't seen me anyway. She's wearing one of the T-shirts she always wears when she's not in school uniform. It's black, with white writing on it. *We are all just people.*

All just people. Well, duh. She started wearing T-shirts like that a couple of years ago. Ones with writing on them. *Humanity not Protectionism. No to Borders.* She's probably got a whole wardrobe full of them. They're pretty ridiculous, in my opinion. It's like Dad says, you have to look out for yourself. Countries have to do the same. If someone's stupid enough to wind up homeless, it doesn't mean they can expect to move in with you. So why should foreigners think they should be able to move here, take our jobs, just because their countries have run out of money? It's not like we've got any to spare. It's not like there are enough jobs for everyone here anyway.

I keep walking. Even though the stone is just under my little toe. Hurts every time I put my right foot down. I curse under my breath, then surreptitiously give my foot a shake. I start walking again – now it's under my big toe. Hurts even more.

It's been an all right afternoon, actually – can of Coke, sitting on a bench by the river. No freaks, so far as I could tell. No one interrupting me or getting in my way.

I could have been working, of course. Doing my assignments, revising for my GCSEs. Could have. Should have, Dad would say. I didn't, though. Not worried about it either.

Not *that* worried anyway. There's always tomorrow. Or the next day. It's not that I don't like school, it's just . . . OK, I don't like it. I don't like the teachers, don't like the way people look at me, the way everyone hangs around in groups that I'm so not interested in being a part of but which make me feel . . . you know, kind of weird, like I don't belong anywhere.

Not that I need to belong anywhere. I'm fine as I am.

I shuffle home, walking on the side of my foot to stop the stone digging in. It's a pointy little thing, more like a nail. I stop again, bang the toe of my shoe into the ground. The stone moves – it's between my big toe and second one now. Tolerable.

A man walks by. He slows down as he approaches me, looks at me, right at me. He looks familiar. He's staring; I force myself not to look at him, to look down at the ground. Freaks, I mutter under my breath. Leave me alone.

My hands are still in my pockets. *You're imagining it. It isn't real.*

A mother walks past with a pram and a toddler. She doesn't look at me. She's engrossed in the small boy, a little smile on her face. He's tottering towards the river and she lets him take a few steps before scooping him up in her arms. She puts him on her hip and continues to push the pram. She hasn't even noticed I'm there. It makes me feel better. Mothers and babies always do – they're consumed with each other, no time to notice me.

It throws me off guard, though. I miss the girl walking towards me. Actually, the girls always catch me off guard. I don't suspect them, especially the pretty ones. Pitiful, isn't it?

This one's older than me – seventeen, maybe eighteen. Long legs, curly hair. She's looking at me and I fall for it, I look back and I think maybe I know her from somewhere. School? Town? But of course I don't. I realise it too late – she's one of them.

She's looking at me intently now and I realise that her eyes have that glazed, hollow look. I try to look away but once they've locked on to you it's hard to break away and I feel like I'm falling, like she's leading me somewhere, but where? I don't know. And then she's passing me and she's still looking but I manage to keep going forward without looking back, kicking myself for letting her suck me in. Or for letting my subconscious suck me in. The shrink said I was imprinting my own desires and fears on to strangers. He said I was looking for my mother. He said I should try to meet more people, not spend so much time alone. He was full of shit. People were the *problem*, that much I knew. I needed to see less of them, not more.

I want to turn around, to look at the girl, to see if she's still looking at me. It's like an itch, like a mosquito bite that you want to scratch and it drives you crazy but you know that even touching it will just make it worse. I don't turn. I know she'll be looking. They always are. I walk faster. I look down at the ground. If I don't think about her, then she won't be real. I list football teams in my head, do the alphabet backwards. I start to run.

I asked Claire once if she saw them. A few years ago when we were still friends. She just looked at me and frowned. If you asked Claire a question that interested her, or that perplexed her, or that she just thought was downright weird, she never looked at you oddly, or took the piss. She always thought hard and then gave a measured response. She never made me feel like a prat.

'Sometimes I see people I think I recognise but I've mistaken them for someone else,' she said.

I nodded. 'Often?'

She frowned again. 'Maybe once every six months? I don't know really.'

I digested this. 'Do you notice people staring at me sometimes? Like really staring when they walk past me?'

She shook her head. 'No, Will, I don't. Are you OK?'

'I'm fine. Don't worry about it.'

They've made me suspicious. The freaks, I mean. Whenever I meet someone new, I look at them aggressively. My dad's sister, who I hadn't seen for years, came to stay unexpectedly and no one warned me. When I got home and she walked towards me with her arms outstretched, I nearly ran out of the house.

I wish I wasn't like that. I wish I was normal.

But what's normal? Is anyone really normal?

I sigh; the stone's back. Under the pad of my foot. I almost like the pain now – it takes my mind off the girl. Am I imagining it then? Do they really exist or is it just my mind playing tricks with me?

If I had the balls, I'd stop them, ask them what the hell they're doing, staring at me. Tell them to take a running jump. I don't have the balls, though. Anyway, if I am imagining it, I'll end up ranting at someone who has no idea what I'm talking about. People already think I'm weird – if I started babbling at strangers I'd be put away. That would tip Dad over the edge. I honestly don't know what he'd do.

I'm startled out of my rambling thoughts by something crossing my line of vision. Someone running. I stop instinctively and move back against the wall next to the pavement. I don't know why; it's like a reflex. I sometimes think I should join the army when I grow up. Or the secret service. I've kind of figured out how to blend into the background, how to keep myself hidden. You could call it prudence, or you could call it not wanting to get into any more trouble than is absolutely necessary. Claire used to call me Shadow Man. She used to tease me about it. Then, later, she said I was shifty. That was around the time she stopped smiling at me, stopped finding me at the end of school to walk home with.

But I'm not being shifty. I'm being cautious.

I edge along the wall to the corner. I'm only two streets away from our house. There's a small parade of shops on the corner – I can see someone on the ground, with another man crouching over him. I think the one on the floor might be drunk, but I'm not sure. Something isn't right about this. I can feel it in my bones.

I move closer. I narrow my eyes, try to focus. If I move, the person crouching might ask for my help. If

I stay here, I won't be noticed – I won't have to do anything.

I frown, trying to work out what's going on. And then I feel my stomach somersault. The man crouching isn't a man at all. It's Yan. I look at him suspiciously. His eyes are wide and he's pulling at something. He's crying out. He sounds weird, sounds scary.

I feel my heart beginning to pound in my chest. I can see what he's pulling at now – it's a knife. Yan's staring at it in shock.

The man on the ground isn't moving. I'm pretty sure he isn't drunk after all. He looks like Mr Best. He's got that green sweatshirt on he wears for work. A woman in a pink sari runs out of the shop, screaming. Mrs Rajkuma. I feel a weird feeling at the base of my spine – not pain, but not *not* pain, if you know what I mean. The body – it's definitely Mr Best, the man who runs the post office in Mr Rajkuma's store. Robber shop, Dad calls it. Open all hours and as expensive as Harrods. Yan is still holding the knife, still looking at it in horror; even from here I can see that it is stained deep red. Mrs Rajkuma is screaming and calling to her husband. Mr Rajkuma comes out of the store; he looks terrified.

'He's been stabbed,' Yan cries out. 'Someone call an ambulance.'

I realise with a jolt that he's seen me, that he's shouting at me. I freeze. He's leaning over the body,

22

holding Mr Best's head. He's breathing into his mouth.

I think about going to help, but know that I won't. Shadow Man doesn't get involved. Shadow Man isn't brave.

'Quick,' Yan shouts. 'He's dying.'

I dig out my phone, but I needn't have bothered. A police car turns up. Three policeman jump out and circle Yan, all pointing guns at his head.

'Drop the weapon,' a policeman shouts. Yan looks confused. He drops the knife.

'You don't understand,' he shouts. 'I just found him. It wasn't me.'

An ambulance arrives; uniformed men and women jump out and put Mr Best on a stretcher, then they wheel him into the ambulance. Mrs Rajkuma is still wailing; a woman tries to comfort her.

The policemen grab Yan and bundle him into the car. He looks back at me. He mouths something. I think it's 'Please help'. I can feel the back of my neck prickling. Then it feels like it's getting dark – from the edges of my vision inwards. Please help. I hear the words in my head, hear them rising, louder, more desperate. I shut my eyes. I need to find the wall, find something to hold on to. My back hits the wall. I'm OK. I take a few deep breaths. I open my eyes.

The car door is closed; it drives off. All that's left is Mr Best's blood on the pavement.

CHAPTER THREE

I don't go home for a while. I can't. I need to process
what I've seen. I feel a bit sick, the kind of sick you
feel when you realise you've done something really
really stupid, or when you realise that you've been
found out over something. That pit of the stomach
sickness that eats away at you until you have to own
up or something because otherwise it'll consume you.

But I haven't done anything stupid. There's nothing
to own up to. I just saw . . . Actually, I don't want to
think about what I saw. Don't want to think about
anything.

'You're late.'

Dad speaks the minute I open the door. I look at
him for a second or two. I want to tell Dad what happened. I want to tell him so he can sort my head out
for me, to make sense of it. But Dad doesn't look like
he's in the mood.

'Late for what?' I say eventually. The television's on. It's the news. My eyes rest on it for a few seconds – there's been a fire at a building housing eastern European workers. Steelworkers, the newsreader is saying. Foul play is suspected. She interviews a man in a suit who says that this kind of action is intolerable, that economic migrants are being scapegoated because of the recession. Then another man comes on, an angry-looking man, who says that the other man doesn't understand the situation, doesn't care about the working man, that this sort of thing will keep on happening until a new government is in place, one that will work to make Britain great again instead of letting us get walked over by anyone and everyone.

'Where have you been?'

I don't hear the question at first; I'm concentrating on the newsreader. Then Dad asks me again and I look up.

'Nowhere.'

'You've been at the river again? You know I don't like you going there.'

'Where else am I going to go?'

'You could stay here and do some work. You could help out round here. Do something useful for a change.'

We stare at each other; we know this could go either way. A normal conversation or a big fight. It doesn't take much these days. I'm not sure why. It's probably my fault.

Me and Dad, we get on. But we're not close. It's not like it was when Mum was here. When she was still alive, there was more . . . I dunno, warmth. We did stuff together as a family. We laughed more. Me and Dad, we're fine, but. I always feel like somehow I'm letting him down.

'There's some chicken in the oven.' Dad sits back on the chair that's been his position in the sitting room since Mum died. They used to sit on the sofa together, but looking at him now I can't imagine it somehow.

No fight then. In some ways I'm disappointed. Sometimes it feels like we only really communicate with each other when we're arguing.

'Thanks.'

I go into the kitchen, take out a plate. It's a ready-meal chicken kiev – I can smell the garlic. I boil some peas; there are chips in the oven too. I hear Dad come in behind me.

'Everything all right?'

I shrug.

'I've got Patrick coming over in a minute or so. Nasty business. Happened earlier this evening. Mr Best from the post office was stabbed.'

I turn my head slightly.

He shakes his head wearily. 'And the government says curbing immigration isn't the answer. What about protecting our own people from those foreign thugs? What about that? Like Patrick says, sometimes people need a shock to make them look around and see what's happening.'

I look at him curiously. He doesn't usually talk to me about this kind of stuff. Usually he just asks me about homework or tells me to stop doing whatever it is I'm doing. Him talking to me like this makes me feel older, like an adult, as if he respects me. I want him to carry on. I like it. I rack my brains for something to say.

'I saw . . .' I say, then stop when his head turns towards me.

'Saw what, son?'

'Nothing.' Wrong thing to say. Why do I always do that?

He's staring at me. 'Nothing? You saw nothing? Come on, son. Out with it.'

I swallow with difficulty. I'm fenced in. I don't have a choice. 'I saw it,' I say. 'I was there.'

'You were there? And you didn't say anything before?'

I look down. 'I didn't . . . I mean, I . . .'

'You saw who did it then?' He's not staring now; he's looking at me closely, almost warily.

'No. I saw Yan . . .'

'Yan.' Dad nods. 'No surprise there.'

He looks away, picks a plate up off the counter.

'No, he wasn't . . .' I start to say, but Dad isn't listening any more.

'Now he's going to know what it feels like,' he's muttering to himself. 'Now he's going to find out.'

'Yan?' I ask uncertainly.

Dad looks as though he's forgotten I was even there.

'Not Yan,' he says. 'That man.'

He means Yan's dad. I'm pretty sure he does anyway. They don't get on. Actually, that's the understatement of the year.

I sit down next to him and start to eat. The inside of the chicken kiev is too hot – it burns my mouth. I get up to pour myself a glass of water.

'I think Yan was shouting for help,' I say eventually. 'He called for me to phone the police.'

Dad turns sharply. 'After he'd seen you,' he says. It's a statement not a question. I nod. I take a gulp of water and feel the relief on my scalded tongue. 'Of course he did,' Dad says. 'Oldest trick in the book. First witness to murder is almost always the guilty party.'

'Mrs Rajkuma was there first,' I say.

Dad's eyes narrow. He's not that big on the Rajkumas either but I don't think even he thinks Mrs Rajkuma's capable of murder.

I should drop it. I know I should. Why won't I? 'It looked . . . It looked like Yan was trying to give Mr Best mouth-to-mouth.'

Dad snorts. 'I bet he was. Look, son, he had Mr Best's money in his pockets. His fingerprints are all over the knife.'

I digest this for a second or two. 'I'm not sure, Dad. It didn't look like he'd done it.'

Dad's fist comes down on the table hard. 'You saw

him there,' he thunders. 'Don't you argue with me about things you know nothing about. They've got the evidence. It's cut and dried. Patrick told me. That little punk is going to get what he deserves.'

I walk back to my stool. I catch Dad's eye, hold his gaze for a few seconds. Then I nod.

Dad doesn't move for a little while. Then his hand moves towards me, awkwardly, and attempts a sort of punch on my shoulder.

'Me and you. We're a team, aren't we, son? We're on the same side, right?'

I look at him curiously. Then I smile. 'Sure,' I nod. 'We're a team.' I finish my chicken kiev and push the plate away.

It was two years before Mum died that Yan and his family moved next door. Patrick told Mum and Dad that it was a sign of the times that only people like them could afford to buy houses these days, but Mum told him to mind his own business and Dad didn't say anything. But I could see Dad was wary of them. When Yan's dad said hello to him on the street, he never looked him in the eye; he just kind of half waved and scooted indoors as quickly as he could.

But that didn't bother me. There were now two boys who lived next door and they wanted to hang out with me. Yan was two years older than me and he had a little brother who was two years younger.

We played football in their garden a couple of

times. Our gardens were side by side and only divided by an old wire fence with huge holes in it, so it was easy for me to go round there. Yan was much better than me, which wasn't ideal, but he taught me some stuff – tricks, exercises. His little brother never said much. Shy, Yan said.

Then his dad invited us all round for supper. Dad didn't want to go but Mum persuaded him. She was good at persuading him to do things. He'd start off all gruff, and Mum would tease him, then she'd ask him questions that he couldn't really answer, like 'Give me one good reason for not going. And don't tell me you've got a headache – you haven't', and then she'd kiss him and tell him that without her he'd be the grumpiest man in the whole wide world and that he should live a little, that maybe he was nervous of saying yes in case he actually enjoyed himself.

It was a warm evening and we sat outside at a table covered in little candles, and ate spicy food in bowls and huge loaves of bread that didn't taste anything like the bread we had at home. I remember it as if it was yesterday, even though I was only six. It felt like we were in another country; the house was the same as ours but it was completely different. I'd been round there once before when it was Mr and Mrs Daniels' house, and then it had been like any other house only a bit more musty, as though no one had opened any windows or washed any clothes in a while. But now that Yan's family lived there it smelt sweet and clean and warm all at once. His mother was really pretty too. Not as pretty as Mum, not the same kind of pretty. She was fatter, but in a nice way, and she had these dark eyes with really long eyelashes and lots of black make up all around them that made her look like a cat or something. She always leant down to my level when she spoke to me and it made me blush, made me want to grow up quickly so that she didn't have to. We ate our meal, Yan's mother showing us how to use our bread to dunk into the various bowls and then using our hands to put it straight in our mouths. And I barely dared to look at Dad, who always said that only savages ate with their hands and who made me use my knife and fork properly, not even just a fork because that was 'American'. Mum winked at me and started to dunk, and then I did and it was delicious, not like anything we ever had at home, and it was spicy and made my cheeks glow. Eventually Dad had some too. And some beer. After a while he actually started to relax – he lost the frozen look off his face and started to talk a bit more normally, like he wasn't counting the seconds until he could leave.

And then Yan's dad spread out his hands and told Dad about the company he'd bought. For a 'knock-down price'. 'So many bargains to be had here,' he said, his eyes twinkling. 'It is the new land of opportunity.'

Dad didn't say anything. I think he wanted to, but Mum gave him one of her looks.

'And great that you did,' she said quickly.

'Otherwise it could have collapsed. Hundreds of people would have lost their jobs.'

'Would have,' Yan's dad agreed. 'Without a doubt.'

'You did all right, though, didn't you?' Dad said, a hint of bitterness in his voice.

'I did very all right.' He didn't notice the bitterness in Dad's voice; he grinned at his good fortune. 'Very happy.'

Then he told us that he was going to be sprucing up the house. Painting it. Redoing the fence, that sort of thing. Mum said that would be great. Said they'd been thinking about doing something to our house too. And then she was grinning too. She looked younger, suddenly, like a girl. I sort of liked it and sort of didn't at the same time. She was giggly and flushed; she'd been drinking wine. I didn't mind that – she always hugged me a lot when she'd been drinking wine. There was music playing softly in the background – a hypnotic rhythm, drums, and an instrument I'd never heard before. It made me feel light-headed. After we'd eaten, she stood up and started to move, just gently, her hips moving from side to side. And Yan's dad got up and took her hand and then they were dancing in the garden, just like that. Dad was staring at Mum like he couldn't believe his eyes. Then Yan's mother asked him if he'd like to dance too. He just kind of shrank back and said no, he didn't dance, thanks all the same. And she winked at me and asked if I wanted to dance instead. And I wanted to so much I was almost bursting, but I said no, because Dad had, because of what he might think, because of how stupid I might look.

Mum looked so happy. Looked as though she didn't have a care in the world.

She sang that night when she put me to bed. Kissed me lots of times, all over my face until I pushed her away but only half-heartedly. I miss Mum. I wish I hadn't pushed her away now.

Patrick arrives at eight o'clock. Dad shows him into the living room and pours him some whisky.

'Go on then. Shouldn't really, Harry,' Patrick says, his eyes looking at him beadily. He always calls dad Harry, even though everyone knows he prefers Henry. And Dad never says anything, even though he'd go mad if anyone else called him that.

Patrick used to be a policeman. A senior one. But he isn't one any more – he's a politician now. He wears a little badge, with a white and red flag on it, and he always makes us go to rallies where he shouts things like *England for the English*, and *British Jobs for British Workers*.

He's been a friend of Dad's for years – they met through work. He used to wear a uniform, years ago. But that was when he was a policeman. He wears another uniform now, though – drab, grey suits and white shirts that stretch against his stomach. He opens his jacket when he sits down – he looks like he's longing to open the top button of his trousers too. I don't know why people don't just buy bigger trousers. Or lose weight. Wearing clothes that are too small just makes you look like a bloater.

Patrick comes round whenever he wants to. Mum never liked him. She used to say he treated our house as if it was his own, bossing her about and helping himself to whatever was in the fridge. Dad would just shrug and say the house might as well be his; without Patrick's help they'd have lost it.

Dad pours another whisky for himself. I eye him warily.

Patrick sits down. 'And how are you, Will? Behaving yourself at school? Haven't been chucked out yet?'

I raise an eyebrow. He always asks the same questions, with a look in his eye that suggests he already knows the answers. 'Not yet,' I say.

'He's doing very well,' Dad says immediately, even though he's got no idea. 'Aren't you, Will?'

There's a pause then, a silence. It's awkward. Patrick looks at me with a half-smile on his face. 'So got some homework to do then?'

It takes me a few seconds to realise this is my cue to leave. Not a bad idea, if Dad's on the whisky.

'Sure,' I lie. Actually, it isn't a lie – I have got homework to do. I just have no intention of actually doing it. Not now anyway.

But I loiter in the doorway. 'You're here about Mr Best? About Yan?'

Patrick looks at me sharply.

'He was there, apparently,' Dad says quickly, in case Patrick thinks he might have discussed the case with me. 'Saw the whole thing.'

Patrick's eyes widen and he looks at Dad, who shakes his head very slightly.

'He saw Yan,' he says. 'Saw him crouching over the body, didn't you, son?'

I nod uncertainly.

'You did, did you?' Patrick says. 'How come we didn't know?'

We. Like he's in charge of the police force. He's not even a policeman any more.

'I didn't hang about. I just saw Yan giving him mouth-to-mouth.'

'Mouth-to-mouth?' Patrick laughs darkly. 'Yeah, that'd be right. He'd just killed the man. He was probably looking for his wallet.'

'Maybe.' I shrug.

'Maybe?' Patrick's eyes narrow.

'He was a long way away,' Dad says. 'He doesn't know what he saw, not really.'

'Still, you'll need to go down to the station. Make a statement,' Patrick says.

I think about this. I don't want to go down to the police station. Even more people asking me if I'm keeping out of trouble, if I'm working hard at school, if I've got a girlfriend. It's like there are only three questions that certain adults can think of when faced with a teenager.

'Do I have to?'

Patrick winks at me. 'How about you tell me what happened and I'll see if it's worth passing it on? How about that?'

I think about it for a second or two, then nod. 'Yeah, OK.'

'So why don't I talk to your Dad first, then come upstairs and find you? What do you say?'

'Fine,' I say. I look at Dad. 'I'll be on the computer.' He opens his mouth but nothing comes out. 'Research,' I say. His mouth closes.

I make my way upstairs to my room, turn my computer on, then, suddenly overcome with fatigue, I throw myself on the bed, allowing my eyes to close. My computer can wait. Right now, sleep can't.

CHAPTER FOUR

I am hot. Too hot. The sun burns my skin. I'm running. The altitude is high; I catch my breath. I'm chewing something. Chocolate. No, not chocolate. Not sweet. It gives me energy. I'm thirsty, but I have nothing to drink. Up and up, like a mountain, but there are steps beneath my feet. I stumble but fear drives me forward, upward. Life or death. Survival or . . . My clothes stick to me, my shoes rub unbearably. I turn a corner, I am near the top. I must reach the top, must get far enough away. I scramble, using my hands now, flailing against the unforgiving clay. I pull, I heave, I push myself up. I am at the top. I am being pursued. I must get away from the mob. I must get away . . .

Another place – here there is a line of people ahead of me. Broken people – thin, frail, slumped, their eyes vacant, a flicker of something here and there but

*mostly they are looking down. For safety. They
shuffle forward; no one speaks. The train behind
them leaves. One or two turn to watch it go. Their
faces are hollow. I reach up to feel my own face; I can
feel nothing. Do I exist? Forward again, bags and
children's hands clutched tightly. There are two piles.
One for clothes, one for bags. Two doors – one for
women and children, one for men. The line inches
forward. One or two people speak, make light of the
situation. It is better, no? Things will improve. Don't
look like that – always so negative. A child cries; his
mother pulls him to her.*

*It is days later. I can smell it. Death. Burning flesh.
It fills my nose, fills my chest, I am choking, splutter-
ing, it is consuming me. I am screaming, screaming,
screaming . . .*

I sit bolt upright, drenched in sweat; it takes me a few
minutes to catch my breath, to slow my heart. I look
around the room, disoriented. I was asleep. I look at
my watch. It's only 9 p.m. I breathe in and out,
slowly. I remember – I came up to play on the computer. Patrick's downstairs with Dad. Did I really
scream? Did they hear me? Maybe they called up to
me? Is that what woke me up?

I lean over the side of the bed, my head between my
knees. Recovery position. Can you recover from
nightmares? What is there to recover from? They're
my own imagination. I do it to myself. The human

brain is a scary thing when you're not in control of it.

The door opens slightly and my father's face appears around it. 'Everything all right, son?' He's drunk. I can tell from the slur in his voice. But he's happy drunk. Otherwise he wouldn't be asking if I was OK; he'd be telling me to shut up, to stop being a freak, so stop being such a bloody disappointment to him.

I nod. 'Yeah. Just . . . got carried away. With a game,' I say lamely, but he swallows it.

'We're just finishing up. Give us a few more minutes.'

'Whatever. Take as long as you want.'

I can't look at him, can't let him see my flushed face, my shaking hands. Always the same nightmares. Sometimes I get the director's cut, sometimes the edited version. Nothing different about them, though – fear, death, torture. I wonder what my old shrink would make of them.

I pull myself up heavily from the bed. Got to calm down before I go downstairs. I look out of the window. A hundred yards away or so I can see Claire's room. There's a light on. That light used to be our signal – Claire used to flash it on and off when her parents had gone to bed and I'd climb out of the window and shin up the drainpipe. We used to talk mainly. She was always very good at listening. We'd listen to CDs too – mostly hers, which were pretty rank in a cheesy kind of way. I'd bring my own round sometimes – try to educate her, try to improve her mind.

Claire was the first person I met when we moved here. I saw her immediately, as soon as I'd got out of the car. Dad told me to wait while the removal van parked, but I saw her out of the window. She was walking right towards us, dawdling like girls do.

I timed it to perfection, waiting for her to be almost next to me before I opened the car door. It nearly knocked her off her feet.

I looked down at the ground; she just looked right at me. That was the thing with Claire – she doesn't act like normal people. She never seems to have any of the hang-ups.

'You the ones moving in here?' she asked, pointing at our house.

I nodded. I was already embarrassed. I was always embarrassed.

'Are you our new neighbour?' That was my mum. 'I'm Chloe and this is William. Will.'

'I'm Claire,' Claire said, looking at my mother curiously.

A woman appeared around the corner. 'Claire!' she said, her tone exasperated. 'Here you are. I've told you before, do *not* walk away from me like that.'

'I didn't walk away,' Claire said seriously. 'You were just walking too slowly.' Even then she wasn't someone you wanted to get in an argument with.

Funny, I remember that like it happened yesterday too. I have a very good memory. Unnerving, Dad calls it. I remember whole conversations word for word, remember what someone was wearing down to the

40

'Country's not what it was, Will. But things are going to change for the better. You just wait and see.'

I nod. I can't imagine what 'better' would look like. Except that the freaks wouldn't be here any more.

'Great,' Patrick says, closing his notebook. 'Well, I'll make sure the police get this. Night, Will. You sleep well, OK?'

CHAPTER FIVE

The following morning I wake, like I always do, feeling like I haven't slept. At least I didn't dream again last night. Two lots of night terrors in twenty-four hours would have been harsh.

I stumble out of bed. My curtains are still open – I find my eyes flickering over to Claire's house; her curtains are closed. I look away.

I'm feeling rough. Slightly nauseous. I think of the night before, of Patrick telling me things were going to change for the better. How? I should have asked. How will they be better?

I pull on some clothes half-heartedly. School day. Great. Just what I need. More rules, more people telling me what to do, stupid imposed routines. When I complained about it to Dad, he just grinned. Wait till you've got a job, he said. Wait till you're on the nine-to-five conveyor belt. Then you'll know about pointless rules. Then you'll know about routine.

I wander into the bathroom and brush my teeth.

I have an uncomfortable feeling in my stomach. Like when I've forgotten something important. Only I haven't forgotten anything – it isn't that. It's . . . It's Patrick. I'm not sure he listened properly. Not sure he heard right. Like when I told him about Yan leaning over the body, giving him mouth-to-mouth. Did I see close up? he asked. I shook my head. You're sure he was giving mouth-to-mouth? I shook my head again. So he could have been rifling through his pockets, could he?

I put down my toothbrush. Who knows. Maybe he was. Like Patrick said, I wasn't that close. Maybe I got it wrong. I told Patrick the facts, and that's what matters. Like he said, it isn't my job to interpret.

But I've still got a bad taste in my mouth.

Then I remember why. It isn't Patrick. It isn't Yan, or Mr Best even. It's the young woman. Last night, in my garden. The freak. I know she was there, know I didn't imagine it. I start to sweat. They're getting closer. Either the freaks are getting closer, or I'm getting madder.

'Don't want to be late for school, son,' a disembodied voice calls up the stairs.

Don't I? How does he know?

'Yeah. Coming.'

I decide against breakfast – instead I clean my teeth again. I look at myself in the mirror. I've got bags under my eyes, dark shadows that make me look a bit

47

like a junkie. Not that I've ever come across a real junkie – just the ones you see on telly. Pathetic, isn't it? Most of my life experience gleaned from programmes made by geeks who work for the BBC.

School is a twenty-minute walk away. It's a good school – well thought of, does OK in the league tables. We had an inspection a year ago and it was like one of those makeover shows – everywhere was painted, Sellotaped together, made to look as shiny as possible. We had to wear our uniform properly, neatly, with NO ABERRATIONS for the whole time they were there; we had to be polite, hold doors open, make out we were responsible, mature individuals who were having a great 'learning experience'. I enjoyed it, actually – took the opportunity to do a bit of role play. I pretended I was someone called Alfred who loves geometry. One of the inspectors interviewed me and I think he was pretty impressed. I said my only criticism of the school was that people didn't take trigonometry seriously enough. He didn't say anything to that; he just nodded and looked at me strangely for a few seconds.

Maybe I should be an actor when I'm older. Are actors all people just trying to escape from who they are?

I walk through the gates. I'm in a sea of navy blue, white and grey. Grey trousers/skirts, white shirts, blue jumpers, blue cardigans, grey jackets. Grey socks, great clunky shoes. It's familiar, reassuring. I can disappear into it, get swept away by the grey, navy and white current.

A familiar smell hits me as soon as I get to the door, as soon as I'm in the corridor. School smell. Cleaning fluids, smelly feet, hormones, desperation, boredom, dirty hair, urine. They did their best to get rid of it for the inspectors – masked it with paint, mainly. But it was back before the week was up. It's soaked into the fabric of the building.

I wander into the boys' toilets. There are several urinals, a few cubicles. You go in one of them at your peril; some idiot's only going to bang on the door while someone else climbs up to see what you're doing, to put you off your stride. It's a jungle, school. You can't let your guard down ever.

I'm done now; I'm at the basin, washing my hands. Don't know why I bother really – the moment I touch anything they're going to be covered in germs again, but you go through the rituals, don't you? Gives life order, or something like that. If you stop believing that washing your hands will make them clean, then you may as well give up on everything.

I'm looking in the mirror again. I'm not vain, don't get me wrong. More interested. My face has changed. Is changing. Gradually, but I only noticed a few weeks ago so it's come as a bit of a shock. My cheeks are hollowing. I don't look so much like a kid any more. I look older. I look weary. Fifteen-year-olds aren't meant to look weary, are they?

I squint at my reflection; I don't know if I like what I see. What do other people see? I try to look at myself objectively. Dark hair. Longish. Straggly. Dad wants me to cut it but I keep avoiding the barbers. I like it long. Curly too. Not corkscrew curls, just a wave. I like to think I've got natural surfer hair.

Actually, that's something Claire once said. She told me my hair suited me – that I shouldn't cut it off because it softened my face. She said my hair was a clue to who I really was. I remember asking how she knew who I really was, and she said that she saw me sometimes, the real me, hidden under all these layers. She said I wasn't that tough underneath. Naturally, I punched her. Not hard, just in protest.

I scrutinise my appearance. Does my face need softening? I narrow my eyes in concentration. I've got blue eyes. Cold blue. Cold blue's intimidating. It can be useful having intimidating eyes, though. I've got quite a square jaw too. That's good, right?

I turn my face to consider my profile. I notice someone looking up at my reflection and I swing round, startled, embarrassed.

It's Yan's brother. He's slumped against the wall. He looks like he's got a broken nose. There's blood all over his face.

I don't know how long he's been there. Didn't hear him come in. Has he been watching me all this time? 'Here. Clean yourself up.' I throw him a paper towel and he dabs uselessly at his nose. 'What happened?'

He shakes his head. 'Nothing. Nothing happened.'

Yan's brother is in Year Eight. He's got none of Yan's easy confidence, none of his footballing skills. He's a bit overweight, which doesn't help, and he gets nervous when he's talking in front of lots of people, even people he knows.

He hangs out with the oddballs in his year. The geek squad, they call them. That could explain the bleeding nose – someone probably punched him. There's a few in every year. The misfits – the ones who are too clever, or too stupid, or just plain weird. He falls into the last category. I guess it's because he's foreign.

'Doesn't look like nothing.' I pass him another wet towel. With his face cleaned up a bit you can see his nose isn't broken, just covered in blood and snot. His eyes look up at me, nervous, afraid.

'You need to watch yourself,' I say. 'Your brother's in enough trouble as it is.'

He nods silently.

'You're sure you don't want to say who did this to you?' I ask. I can't help the guy if he won't tell me who punched the living daylights out of him.

He shakes his head again.

'Suit yourself.'

The door bangs behind him. I move to leave the bathroom but images of Yan, of Mr Best, of the freak woman, come into my mind and I feel light-headed suddenly. I hold on to the basin, steadying myself. My head hurts. I breathe in and out slowly. I tell myself to stop thinking about Yan. Like Dad said last night when I asked him about my statement, I need to leave the police work to the police and legal stuff to the lawyers. They're trained. They know what they're doing. I've done my bit.

I realise I didn't get any lunch money off Dad. I'm starving – my lack of breakfast is starting to look like a pretty stupid idea. I'm feeling nauseous again. Maybe I'm coming down with something. I put my hand in my pocket hopefully – maybe I left a quid in there last week. Unlikely but you never know. My hand alights upon a piece of paper. A receipt? Some useless note? I pull it out and my eyes light up. A fiver. I've just found a fiver in my pocket.

I'm smiling now. Doesn't take much for life to feel much better, does it? Now I can grab something from the canteen before school starts. Seek and ye shall find. Just when you think life is going down the pan, you get enough of a break to think that maybe things aren't so bad, just for a little while.

It's nearly lunchtime. I've got through double Science; now I'm in History. Half an hour until lunch. Thirty minutes. 1800 seconds. Tick, tock.

It's funny, time. I mean you'd think, really, that it's just constant, that it doesn't change. But it does. It speeds up, slows down; sometimes it disappears completely. If you could control it, if you could make time do what you wanted it to do, that would be amazing. Forget Superman or Spiderman – they're pointless, stupid. But Time Man? That would be something. Just to be able to stop sometimes, stop everything. Fast-forward over the rubbish bits, let the good times last for ever.

Me, I'd reverse time. I'd go back a few years. And then I'd press Stop.

'Hodge, perhaps you'd like to tell us what the turning point of the Second World War was?'

Caught, rabbit in the headlights. The teacher saw me looking at the clock. Such a rookie mistake. I grimace.

'It was that battle, wasn't it, Miss?'

She's too clever for that. 'That battle? Could you be more specific?'

I look down at my book. It isn't even open at the right page – it's a chapter about the Russian Revolution.

'D-Day?' I ask, dredging the memory from somewhere. A television programme. I can see black and white images of men jumping off boats. I saw an old film once about a man who knew about the secret landing. He woke up in a hospital after his plane went down and there were all these nurses and nice people looking after him. They said he'd been in a coma. Said the war was long over. Said Britain had won. They were trying to get him to reminisce, to tell them the story about how they wanted the Germans to think they were landing in one place when actually they were landing somewhere else. And then he realised that he had a paper cut on his finger. A paper cut that he'd had the morning his plane went down. D-Day hadn't happened yet. He'd been captured by the Germans and they were trying to find out the real landing destination. For an old film, it was actually pretty good.

'D-Day was how we won the war,' she's saying. 'But there were several turning points during the war. Have you heard of Pearl Harbor?'

I frown. 'Maybe.' I get a weird sensation in my stomach. A kind of tingling in my head. I concentrate on my breathing.

'Maybe.' The teacher rolls her eyes. 'Has anyone else heard of Pearl Harbor? Would someone like to explain what happened and why it changed the course of the war?'

There was a film called *Pearl Harbor* too, wasn't there? I didn't see it. I'm pretty sure of it. I didn't watch it – the football was on at the same time and Dad never likes to miss a match. I think the film was a love story – I didn't know it was about the Second World War.

No one volunteers the answer so the teacher gives up and tells us. It was the Japanese, bombing American bases, making the Americans want to join the war. I'm getting a headache. I think I'm hungry. A Snickers bar probably wasn't the best breakfast.

'And the other turning point was the Battle of Britain,' she's saying. 'Who can tell me something about the Battle of Britain?'

Claire puts up her hand. 'It was the bombing, wasn't it?'

'That's right. A sustained effort by the Luftwaffe to gain superiority over the Royal Air Force. Had the effort been successful, well, the war could have taken a very different turn. As it was, the lack of success was considered a major turning point. Although the destruction wreaked on both sides was devastating.'

'It nearly worked,' I say. I sound angry. I feel angry. It's my head: it hurts. It's making me bad-tempered.

The teacher is staring at me. 'Yes, Hodge. It did. It very nearly worked.'

I nod curtly. She's looking at me strangely; she's not used to me contributing. Nor am I. I don't even know why I said that. I look back at my book. My head is giving me some serious pain. Dehydration maybe. I put my hand to my forehead; I think I can feel it throbbing. I grit my teeth.

'But luckily it didn't,' she continues. 'Luckily we defeated them.'

My head is killing me. I am suddenly full of rage. The teacher is stupid. Ignorant. I dislike her. I despise her.

'OK then,' the teacher is saying. I hear her, but it is like an out-of-body experience. My pain is all I can comprehend. 'Well, that's a start anyway. We're going to be studying this period of history for the next few weeks, and by the end I'll expect you to know every battle, every strategic alliance and the ramifications of these alliances. We'll be looking at the rise of Nazi Germany, the Holocaust, the involvement of Russia, of Poland . . .'

I feel like someone's got a red-hot poker and is sticking it right between my eyes. I put my head on my desk.

'Hodge? Hodge, are you all right?' I should look up, tell her I'm OK, but I don't feel OK. I don't feel at all OK. I want to thrash out.

I focus, force myself to box the emotion safely away. Then I slowly, painfully lift my head off my hands. Open my eyes. The lights are so bright. I can see Claire looking at me, worried, curious. I hold her eye for a few seconds. I look away first.

'I need some water,' I tell the teacher.

She looks at me suspiciously, then nods. I can feel my face is hot, red. A trickle of sweat is making its way down the back of my neck. When I stand up, I realise my shirt is sticking to my back. I pull on my blazer to hide it. I look down at the ground; I need to get out of the classroom as quickly as I can. I run to the boys' toilets, splash my face. Then I walk back down the corridor, pausing at the vending machine to buy myself a can of Coke. I press it to my cheek first, cooling myself. I open it, drink it in one. The effervescence, the sugar-hit, the cold, all at once, make an intoxicating cocktail. I feel better immediately. Not completely normal, but the headache is receding. I can think again. The sweating has stopped.

I lean back against the vending machine, trying to make sense of everything, trying to work out what just happened.

I breathe in and out slowly. My mind feels like it

has exploded and is now gradually coming back together, bit by bit like a jigsaw puzzle. Calmer. The pain has gone. I'm not angry now. I don't know why I was angry. I can't remember. Nothing seems to makes sense. The pieces swim together. I don't know if they are in the right place – it doesn't seem important.

Things don't make sense, but that doesn't really surprise me. *Life* doesn't make any sense. If it did, Mum wouldn't be dead, there wouldn't be people starving in Africa.

None of it's rational. None of it strikes you as something well thought out, organised, put together. It's all just a mess. All just a mass of confusion.

The trick is to accept it, to watch and learn, like the man in the film. Don't give anything away, just in case. Keep your cards close to your chest.

I decide I've had enough school for today. I slope off down the corridor and out into the fresh air.

CHAPTER SIX

I start towards the river then change my mind and head into town. It's always a bit of a gamble choosing where to go when you bunk off. There are fewer people by the river but it's easier to blend in on the high street; I'm less likely to get accosted by someone asking why I'm not at school. The uniform doesn't help. If someone stops me, I usually say I'm researching an Ordnance Survey map for geography. I don't think I've ever convinced anyone but they don't know how to respond to that so I get left alone.

I feel like I'm being watched. Paranoia? I pause outside an estate agent's and turn slowly, like I could just be looking around idly deciding which way to go. There's a woman behind me, walking towards me. She looks like the woman who was in my garden. I feel myself stiffen. I stare at her; she's looking at me. But is it because she *is* the woman, because she's following me, or is it because I'm staring at her? It's hard to know. She walks past me, then she's gone. I turn back to the estate agent's window. I'm sweating again. It's happening – I'm actually going mad. I'm scared. I'm really, really scared.

I try to slow my breath. It's in your head, Hodge. It's all in your stupid head.

That's the thing with emotions. They don't exist. Like the freaks. If you can push them to one side, if you can ignore them, refuse to acknowledge them, then you can get on with stuff, then you can live. But if you don't, if you let them in, they consume you, don't they? You see it on television, people breaking down, people losing it. I don't ever want to lose it. I'm afraid of what would happen if I did. Better to be in control.

So that's what I do. What I've always done.

Well, not always.

Not before Mum . . .

I cried at her funeral. That was the last time. And once I started, I felt like I'd never stop, like my insides were overflowing and cascading down my face. I thought I'd get swept away. I wanted to get swept away, wanted to drown, like her, to be with her, to be safe again.

Mum always made me feel safe. Like a raft, like a pair of armbands. I didn't know it when she was here, didn't notice it. But as soon as she was gone, I felt it. Suddenly I was exposed, vulnerable. But not any more. Now I've got my own armour. Now it's been so long since I cried, I'm not sure I even know how to.

Slowly, gingerly, I start to walk again. Ignore the freaks and they'll go away. They don't exist. I can do this. Just walk straight ahead.

I'm walking towards a man. He's looking at me strangely. Because I look weird? Because I'm sweating, my hands in fists, looking around like a freak? Or because he's one of them? I meet his eyes – they're like hers. Pained. Mournful. I turn around and start to run. I'm losing my mind and I can't stop it, I can't do anything about it. I want them to go away. I want them to leave me alone.

I run into the shopping centre, find a bench, sit down. I breathe – in, out, in, out. Children are playing on a Bob the Builder car thing that jigs up and down. They laugh ecstatically, beg their mothers for another go when it's finished. No one's looking at me. There's a woman selling flowers who barely gives me a second glance. I'm just sitting on a bench, like a normal person.

Not *like* a normal person. I *am* a normal person.

'I'm normal,' I mutter to myself. 'Everything is normal.'

And then I see the girl. The girl with curly hair who was down at the river. She's walking towards me. I'm certain it's her. My heart stops. Who am I trying to kid? Things aren't normal at all. My nails are digging into my palms. I can't look away. I'm imagining it. Of course I am. She's just a girl, that's all, a girl who happens to be walking right towards me. She sits down on the bench next to me. I'm frozen; I can't move, can't think, can't do anything. She's just sitting there, looking at me. She's not making a phone call or reading a magazine; there's no reason for her to be sitting on this bench, on my bench, when there are others free. She saw me and she came and sat down. And now she's sitting there, inches away.

I can't look at her.

I have to look at her.

I take a breath. I want it to be a deep breath but it isn't, it's shallow; my lungs won't take in more air than they need for survival. I turn.

Her eyes look like *their* eyes. I'm not imagining it. I can't pretend this isn't happening. She's looking right at me. I'm staring back. Like I know her . . .

She leans towards me. 'So it *is* you.'

'Look.' My voice sounds too high, too strained. 'Look, I don't know who you are, or what you want, but you have to leave me alone. OK? Just leave me alone. Stop following me. Stop looking at me. Stop acting like you know me. OK? OK?'

I meant to tell her, not ask her. Why am I asking if it's OK?

'But I *do* know you.'

I stare at her angrily. 'No, you don't. You don't know me. I don't know you. Just . . . Just go away.'

I get up and start to walk away, angrily, desperately. When I'd daydreamed about confronting the freaks, I'd imagined them laughing at me for being an idiot, or looking at me strangely because actually they weren't following me or looking at me at all, it was in my imagination. Sometimes I'd imagine them disappearing in a puff of smoke because I'd had the courage to look them in the eye and tell them to go. This, though ... I wasn't prepared for this; for her acknowledging me, saying she knows me, for her actually being real.

'Will. It is Will, isn't it?'

I look behind me and quicken my pace. She's following me. She's trying to keep up with me – I can hear her heels clattering. I'm going to call the police. I'm going to run into a shop and get help.

Help for what? Because an eighteen-year-old girl is following me? Even now my sarcastic mind is laughing at me. Yeah, the police will just love that. They'll put it right to the top of their 'to do' list.

I jump on the escalator, take the steps two at a time. I look around wildly – there's a bookshop. I dive inside, make for the Philosophy section. It's empty – obviously no one reads philosophy books. I lean over and put my hands on my knees, let the blood return to my head.

'I'm sorry. I didn't mean to scare you.'

I stand bolt upright. She's there, right next to me. How did she find me? I feel like I've been transported to some alternative reality. Any minute now the secret cameras are going to appear and someone is going to explain what the hell is going on.

'You didn't scare me,' I say, mustering all the courage I can. She's a girl, not a big bloke. I know judo. I could totally take her down if I needed to. 'You're just really annoying me. Go and follow someone else, OK? Whatever it is you want, I'm not interested.'

'You really don't recognise me, do you?'

She looks perplexed, worried. She looks older up close. Or maybe it's just her eyes – that soulful look they have. Maybe she's part of a cult, I think suddenly. Maybe this is how they get new members – follow them until they're so freaked out they think they need salvation.

I decide I need to take the upper hand. I put my hands on my hips.

'No,' I said, 'I don't *know* who you are. I don't *care* who you are. So you tell all your weird friends I'm not going to fall for it, OK? I'm not interested.'

'Interested in what?'

They're clever these cult people, but they won't get the better of me.

I shoot her a knowing look. 'In whatever,' I say pointedly. 'In whatever it is you want.'

That'll do it. There's no comeback from that. But she doesn't give up.

'I've been looking for you for years. So have the others. When I heard . . . heard you were here, I didn't believe it. Then they said you weren't . . .' She sighs, looks at me worriedly. 'You really don't recognise me? You're sure?'

She looks at me again, those eyes doing the weird thing they did on the bench, looking into mine, like really into them. I feel self-conscious. I feel strange. I feel like I'm remembering something.

I kick myself. That's what she wants me to think. It's like those healers who pretend to make people who are paralysed think they can walk. It's a con. I'm not falling for her rubbish.

'How,' I say, 'could I know you? I've never met you before. Apart from when I saw you the other day.'

She looks away, like she's planning her next move. I start to walk away; she reaches out and grabs my arm. Fear pricks at me. She pulls me close.

'You don't know who you are.' It's not a question. She's shaking her head. 'I don't understand. I don't know how this could happen.'

'No? Well, maybe you've got the wrong person,' I say. 'I've got to go now. I'd like to say it was nice meeting you, but . . .'

I don't finish the sentence. My narky little comment doesn't feel appropriate now. She looks as though she's going to cry. Is it another tactic? Doesn't matter either way. I'm out of here. I'm about to run out of the shop, when I stop, hesitate. Who does she think I am? Shouldn't I find out? She and her friends have been wrecking my life. I should find out who they are, find out as much as I can so that I can do something to get them off my back. Otherwise they might just keep following me. Otherwise it might never be over.

I look at her, catch her eye. Is this something I'm going to regret? Was this all part of her plan? In a week will I be holed up with all those freaks with the eyes in some weird cult place where I have to take ten wives and pray to an alien?

'Look,' I say. 'Tell me what's going on. Tell me why you're following me. Tell me who you think I am. Maybe I can help you find the right person.'

I don't know why I said that. The last thing I want to do is help her. It's just that she looks so . . . broken. It makes me feel bad for her, even if she and her friends have been screwing with my head. Maybe she's depressed like Mum was. Maybe it's her head that's fried, not mine.

She shakes her head. 'I don't . . .' she mutters. 'I can't . . . If you don't remember, I don't know how . . .'

'Remember what?' I ask patiently. I'm in control now. This is better. This I can do. She's the freak, not me. 'What's the problem?'

She looks up at me. 'If you don't know who you are, if you don't know what you are . . . I don't know what I can do.'

Her voice is breathy. I wonder briefly what someone listening in on this conversation would think. I wish someone was; I want corroboration that it's actually happening.

'OK,' I say. 'Well, why don't you try telling me who you *think* I am. Maybe I can clear up the confusion.' I've adopted that patient, patronising tone I've heard Patrick use. The tone he uses with me most of the time. I shake myself.

'Clear up the confusion?' She looks irritated. 'You really think I've got the wrong person?' She shakes her head again. 'You really don't know, do you?' She sighs. 'You can't.'

'Know what?' I'm getting irritated now. 'And stop saying I don't know, like I've forgotten or something. I haven't forgotten anything. I've got a great memory. I never forget anything.'

'You don't?' Her head shoots up. 'What do you mean?'

I blanch slightly. I wasn't exactly telling the truth just then. But she doesn't need to know that – it'll only encourage her. 'Just don't tell me I can't remember you. If I knew you, I'd remember. OK?'

'OK.' She nods, bites her lip. Then she looks around. 'I should go.'

'You're not going to tell me anything?' I ask.

She shakes her head. 'I don't know where I'd even start.'

I glance over at her and catch her eye. There's something about her expression, something incredibly sad but really warm too. Comforting almost. I feel myself softening. Feel myself drawn to her suddenly.

Then I kick myself. She's manipulating me. Her eyes aren't warm; they're strange. *She's* strange. I look down at my hands.

'Are they all with you? All the people who've been following me? With the weird eyes?'

'Weird eyes?'

I feel bad. Like I've insulted her. I don't know why but I don't want to insult her. She looks like she's been through enough.

'Not weird,' I find myself saying. 'Just . . . I dunno. Sad. They've all got sad eyes.'

She smiles. 'Yes,' she says, 'I suppose we have.'

'So there's a we?' I press her. 'You're all in this together?'

'There are . . . a number of us,' she says carefully.

'And you all got it into your head that I was someone you knew?' That film *The Matrix* pops into my mind. Maybe they think I'm Neo. Maybe I've misjudged this whole situation. Maybe they think I'm their saviour. I could be the head of their cult. I could be the godlike figure they worship.

'We didn't get anything into our heads,' she says impatiently. 'You are one of us. You are a Returner. You've been off the grid for years – we were getting worried. And now you're here and you . . . you don't remember.' She looks up at me with those eyes again and I know suddenly that even if this is *The Matrix*, even if they want me to be their leader, I don't want to be. I've heard enough.

'Yeah, well, you got it wrong,' I say hurriedly. 'I'm not a . . . whatever it is you said. I'm me. Will. And I'm not getting involved.'

'You're a Returner, Will. It's what you are,' she calls after me, but I'm not listening as I stride quickly out of the shop.

CHAPTER SEVEN

I've googled Returners. There's no such thing.

Of course there's no such thing.

Actually, that's not strictly true. There are Returners – women returning to work, student returners, returners to research fellowships, returners to teaching. I think we can safely assume I'm none of those things.

I tried Wikipedia too, just to be on the safe side. It says the Returners are part of a game called *Final Fantasy VI*. They're a resistance movement dedicated to the defeat of the Empire. Final Fantasy. That's about right.

Anyway, it's been a while now – ten days, maybe eleven – and I haven't seen a single freak, haven't had anyone following me at all. I think maybe they've realised I'm not going to fall for their crap. I think maybe they've moved on to someone else.

Poor sucker.

Mind you, I can't talk. I'm at school again, in a History lesson. I'm sitting at the back, though. Virtually hidden, counting the seconds until it's over like I always do. There's something about History that I really hate. I didn't want to do it for GCSE but Dad said I had to, insisted I take 'serious' subjects. So I'm sitting here, counting, waiting for it to end, waiting for the door to open, for freedom to beckon for just a few minutes.

Sometimes it feels like all I'm doing is trying to get through the day. Like I'm wishing it all away. Is that what life is? Just getting from A to B, getting from 7 a.m. to 11 p.m. and hoping that nothing's going to go seriously wrong in that time? That's how it is for me. I get a sense of relief every day when I get into bed, like I've done it, got through another one. For what? Where's the eventual prize? What's the eventual point?

And what if Dad's right – what if this is the good bit and work is where it all starts to go seriously wrong? Surely there must be a bit in the middle. A bit that makes everything else worthwhile, a bit that makes you go, 'Ahhhh, so that's what I've been working towards. That's what this is all about,' just before it all goes pear-shaped again. Otherwise why would people bother? Why *do* they bother? Did Mum have the right idea? Did she get a flash of the truth, and realise that the middle bit doesn't exist, that it's all a con? Is that why she . . .

I pull my mind away from that line of thought. The teacher's talking. We're still on the Second World War. She showed us a film on the Holocaust last week, only I didn't watch it – I had a migraine.

'. . . which is why I want you to think about how it would feel – actually feel – to be on the train, knowing what awaits you. Will, you weren't here last week. Why don't you start us off? Tell us what you think it would be like to be a Jew in Nazi Germany. What it would be like to be persecuted like that.'

I look up in horror. I'm at the back. Which everyone *knows* is where you sit when you aren't interested, when you haven't done your homework, when you don't know and don't care what the teacher is going on about. Picking on me is out of order. Why me? Why now? It's nearly the end of the lesson. I look at her sullenly. 'Persecution? I imagine it would feel like this,' I say, regretting the words as soon as I've said them.

The teacher doesn't think it's funny. She hates me, my History teacher. My first lesson with her, we got into an argument. I suppose I was a bit aggressive. I don't know why; she just brings out the worst in me. She's one of those superior types, patronising old women who think they've seen it all before. She told my dad at parents' evening that I shouldn't be doing History if I wasn't interested in it, that I should find another subject. Which was music to my ears except Dad told me I'd better start being interested. Didn't happen, of course.

'If this is what you call persecution,' she says, her voice low, 'then you are very lucky. Many other people are not so lucky. My grandparents were not so lucky.' She's staring at me now, her eyes narrowing. 'So think, Will. I want you to stand up and tell me how it would feel, to have your humanity taken away from you bit by bit, to know that all paths lead to the gas chamber.'

How dare she talk to me like that? Like I'm stupid. How dare she patronise me in front of everyone. My head starts to throb. It gets worse every second, like something piercing right into my brain. I clutch my forehead. Images are flashing through my head. Horrible images. Haunted eyes, gaunt frames, the stench of death, the dust . . .

'Another migraine?' The teacher looks at me with disdain. 'How very fortunate. Are you method acting, Will?'

I remove my hands. Everyone's looking at me. It's all I can do to keep my eyes open. I want to scream, to cry out, but I manage to keep a lid on it. I won't let her have the satisfaction of seeing me suffer.

She shakes her head wearily. 'You know, you're pathetic, Will. Really pathetic. I'm sick of your excuses. I'm sick of you thinking that the rules don't apply to you. Someone else. Rory. You do what Will has failed to so miserably.'

Rory pushes back his chair. She is dismissing me. She will not dismiss me, I won't allow it. I am angry. I am insulted. My eyes narrow as I stare at her. She is

71

pathetic, I tell myself. A teacher. I feel nothing but contempt for her.

'I guess if I were –' Rory starts to say.

'You want to know how it feels to be persecuted?' I interrupt. A sarcastic smile is now playing on my lips.

'I wanted to know how it *would* feel,' she corrects me icily. She has not recognised my anger yet. She will. She will see. Everyone will see. 'But now I've asked Rory. You have to put yourself in someone else's shoes to do this. It's called empathy. Come on, Rory.'

I look at her levelly. Rory opens his mouth to speak.

'Empathy is weakness,' I say. Rory's mouth closes again.

'Weakness? I'm sorry, did I just hear you correctly?'

She is staring at me in surprise. She didn't expect that. She expected me to crumple. I will never crumple. She, on the other hand . . . I look her up and down. She is weak. I know it. I can see it. Under pressure I'd give her seconds, perhaps a minute. She would give in.

How do I know this? I don't know. I don't care.

I say nothing. She will fill the void. Let her. Let her talk herself into her fate. Strength in silence.

'So you want to answer my questions now, Will?' she asks. 'Come on then. You're on a train. You're headed for Auschwitz. You have a child with you, a child you know won't survive. How do you feel, Will? You think it's weak to put yourself in someone else's shoes? You think it's weak to imagine their pain?'

The pain is getting worse. It feels as though my head's going to split in two – red, white, flashing, dark. I clench my fists and push it away. Let the white rage take over. Pain is for the weak. I take a deep breath. My eyes narrow. My cold blue eyes.

'It's a simple question, Will. Imagine how the Jews on those trains must have felt. Imagine how the immigrants who burnt to death here in the UK last week felt. How would you feel if you were suddenly turned upon by people you thought were your friends, your neighbours? Because that's what happened. And that's what's happening here in some parts of the country. Can anyone else give me an example? Hodge, since you're standing up. Can you give me an example?'

She isn't just my teacher any more. She is everything I hate. She is crass, meaningless authority.

I feel my eyes harden, locking on hers. I take a deep breath and formulate a sentence that will silence her.

'Yan,' Claire says suddenly, before I can speak. She is standing up, her eyes flashing. 'He's been arrested for something he didn't do. Just because he's not . . . Just because he's . . .'

'An immigrant?' the teacher asks. Her tone is softer. I feel my nails digging into my palms. Words disappear from my head as the agony returns. Claire's voice has brought back the pain. The ice is melting. I try to concentrate, to bring it back, but it's too late. The teacher is no longer an ogre; she is my teacher again.

'The National Party,' Claire continues. 'All those television ads about sending immigrants back home. That's the same thing. Isn't it?'

I feel my stomach clench. The National Party. Patrick's party. My dad's a member. England for the English. They don't belong here. Send them home. British jobs for British workers. I have searing pain behind my eyes.

A voice in my head. *The Jews are taking over. They will run the world if we let them. They are dangerous. We must protect our people from them. We must stand up for ourselves.* I frown. I remember the words, but from where? Who spoke them? Where did they come from?

I have been running from them. Running for so long.

But running where? I don't understand. Why was I so angry? Where did the hatred come from? I am still angry. I am losing control.

'It is the same thing,' the teacher is saying. 'In times of crisis, we look for someone to blame. It is no coincidence that the rise of the Nazi Party in Germany followed a great depression, a time of utter poverty that resulted from the First World War. And it is no coincidence that the rise in Nationalist politics across Europe has come at a time of economic hardship. It just shows how quickly people can descend into unthinkable prejudice and hatred when their livelihoods are at stake, when they feel threatened. What about Rwanda? Can anyone tell me what happened there?'

Rwanda. My head pounds. A memory. A nightmare. The voice again. I can't get rid of it.

I cannot watch. I am safe here; I don't want to know, don't want to see. That could have been me. Should have been me. If I'd gone back. But I didn't. And I won't. I will not go back. I will hide. I can't go back. Not any more. Too much. The screaming. The ash, the smell, the eyes ... Especially her eyes. The way she looked at me. She knew. She looked at me and her baby cried. She tried to hand it to me. The pain in her eyes, the desperation. I saw it. I felt it. The ice cracked. She got in. She is in me. The pain ... she is the pain, she is the agony that consumed me, that consumes me still. I can't any more. Let someone else do it. Let me stay here, away from it all. Let me not go back ...

Back where?

'The genocide,' someone says. 'The Hutus turned on the Tutsis and massacred them.'

'Their friends and neighbours,' the teacher nods. 'Hacked to death with machetes. Thousands and thousands. Because the Hutus had been led to believe that the Tutsis were to blame for everything that was wrong with their lives. But were they? Were the Jews a malevolent force in 1930s Germany? Are immigrants responsible for the economic collapse of our country?'

'No,' everyone says. All I can hear is Claire's voice. 'No.' She is talking to me. Directly to me. I feel her eyes on me. I feel the freak girl's eyes ...

'No,' I shout. 'No!' I scream. 'Noooooooooo!'

I run to the door, hurl it open. I feel as though I'm suffocating. I have to get some air.

I get outside. I breathe, in and out, in and out. The pain is receding. I feel embarrassed suddenly. I allowed myself to lose it.

But at least I didn't cry.

I walk to the bike shed, find my usual resting place behind it. Someone has left a packet of cigarettes with a lighter inside. I pick it up. Mum always hated the idea of me smoking. Then again, she isn't here, is she? I take out a cigarette and light it, breathing in deeply.

I exhale slowly, watching the smoke dissipate into the air, wishing actions were the same, would just blend into thin air and disappear.

I finish my cigarette and stub it out, lean back, take a deep breath. I'd like to go to sleep, like to curl into a ball, bury myself under a duvet. I briefly consider going home, then rule it out. Dad might find out. Can't risk it. I can't go back into school either, not for another fifteen minutes, not if I don't want to get stopped in the corridor and sent to the head's office. I don't want to go back full stop, but I guess I don't really have a choice.

I don't want to go back.

I remember saying these words before. In a memory. A dream? *I don't want to go back. I won't. I can't.* Who was I speaking to? It doesn't matter.

I close my eyes. Fifteen minutes. It isn't long. The

sun's shining – its rays have found their way through the bike shed to land on my arms, my face, like little torches. Time goes past. I'm warm, I'm comfortable. I remember dappled sunlight, a mellow breeze. Someone stroking my head. Mum? She's soothing me. Everything will be OK. What happened in class made no sense. My reaction followed no logic. It must have been a dream. If I decide it didn't happen then it will be erased.

I stretch, open my eyes again. It takes me a while for my eyes to focus, to realise that Yan's brother is lying next to me. I didn't hear him arrive. I look at him suspiciously.

'What are you doing here?' I ask gruffly.

He looks up – he has dirt on his face, a swollen eye. 'Jeez,' I breathe out. 'You look terrible.'

He appears embarrassed, pulls his hands up to hide his face. I shake my head. He must go looking for trouble – it's easy enough to avoid it if you try. Keep your head down, avoid certain people. The boy must have a death wish.

'You don't learn, do you?' I ask. He looks down.

I don't want to know what happened. Not really. But I ask anyway.

'Piss someone off, did you?'

He shakes his head. 'No.'

I shrug. Dad says Yan's whole family don't belong here. He says they're thieves. 'Must've done. Someone's given you a great little shiner. Must've upset them.'

He shakes his head more vehemently. 'No one did this,' he says.

'No one.' I nod. 'OK.'

He is sitting now; painfully, he pulls himself up to standing.

I feel like I need to say something. He looks so pathetic. Like an injured animal.

'Sorry about your brother,' I say. I'm an idiot for even mentioning Yan. I should have just let him leave, should have kept my mouth shut.

His eyes widen, his lips start to tremble. 'You're not sorry. He's a dirty foreigner.'

He looks scared after he speaks, like he didn't mean to. His eyes widen.

'You said it,' I say. Although I'm surprised. Weird way to describe your own brother.

His head shoots up. He looks scared. 'I'm sorry,' he says.

'No need to be sorry.' I shrug.

He says nothing. But he doesn't go either.

'So how is he? All right?' I'm just making conversation now, filling the space.

'I don't know. I haven't seen him. My father . . . He has been to the prison. He won't let me go. Me and my mother. He says it is a bad place.'

'Yeah, I guess it's pretty bad,' I say uncomfortably. 'But that's what you get for killing someone, right?'

'He didn't kill no one.'

There's a defiance in Yan's brother's eyes that I haven't seen before.

I shrug again. 'Maybe. Didn't look like it from where I was. But the police seem pretty sure, don't they?'

'You were there?' He's looking at me incredulously.

I look back at him blankly and he edges away. I'm relieved. I don't want to have this conversation.

'See you then,' I say.

His eyes cloud over and he nods, then turns and runs.

I look at my watch. It's already the end of morning lessons. Time has fast-forwarded in a good way. Must be the sunshine. I put my hand in my pocket. I pull out 50p along with a piece of paper. I grin. It's a fiver. Another fiver I don't remember. I'm getting good at this. Time for lunch, I think.

The canteen is a low, red brick building that's tacked on between the science block and the main school. It's a jarring sight – the school is Victorian, old yellow brick, tall, imposing, gothic even. Then there's the squat canteen with small windows out of which the smell of burger fat spills. I survey the queue, which is wending its way along the wall and out into the courtyard outside. There's always a kink in the corner – with a bit of clever manoeuvring it's usually a good place to queue-jump. Once I'm in, I wander over, peer at the sausage rolls in their clear plastic cabinets.

'You want one of those?' one of the dinner ladies asks with a sigh. I turn my head a fraction – behind me is a group of girls, two years below me, absorbed in giggles about something.

'Yeah,' I nod. 'With chips and beans.' Pushing the boat out here, I think to myself. I take the plate greedily, put it on a tray. Maybe I was wrong when I said you didn't need more than lemonade in hot weather. I'm starving. I pay and look for a table. There's an empty one, down in the far corner. I head there, put my tray down, then realise I've forgotten to pick up any cutlery. I look at my plate. I could take the tray with me and risk losing the table, or I could leave it, save the table but risk losing my food. I curse myself inwardly – so stupid. Could I eat with my fingers? Steal cutlery from someone else?

'You need a fork?' I turn around, my heart lifting at the sound of Claire's voice. Then I redden, I'm not sure why. She's holding out a fork. 'I noticed you didn't pick one up.'

I frown. 'I didn't . . .'

'Didn't see me? No. You were in another world.'

'Aren't you meant to be in French?' I regret the words as soon as I utter them. Why do I know her timetable? Now she'll know I do.

'Teacher's off sick. We were meant to sit there reading *Le Grand Meaulnes*. Which doesn't strike me as the best possible use of our time. I've read it twice already.'

It's so long since I last spoke to Claire I don't know what to say. Don't know how to act. I take the fork. 'Thanks.'

She eyes my table. 'You sitting here?'

I nod. 'You want to join me?'

'Sure.'

And then she's sitting down opposite me like it's perfectly normal, like two years haven't passed since we last made proper eye contact, as if it's all just disappeared like the smoke: evaporated, dissipated, forgotten.

CHAPTER EIGHT

The truth? I used to be in love with Claire. The sort of love that consumes you – hopeless, soft, vulnerable love. I wanted her to be there all the time. She just had this way of listening to me, putting her hand on mine, all soft and warm, not like Dad who would punch me on the shoulder if he touched me at all. I can't put it into words without sounding like a sap. She had this way of making me feel ... cherished. That's what it was. Sad, right?

Like I said, it was a long time ago when I was younger. A lot of water has passed under the bridge since then. Loads of the stuff. And to be honest, not having her around has had its advantages. I mean, she's difficult, Claire. She used to contradict me, argue with me, challenge me. All the time. She'd never just accept what I said, never just let an opinion be expressed – she had to question it, analyse it, suggest alternative viewpoints. Basically, she complicated everything. Like I said before, she was difficult. Still is, probably.

'So you were there. You saw what happened.'

I looked up sharply. News travels fast. Did Yan's brother run straight to Claire? I berate myself silently for saying anything.

'Saw what?' I say. I feel deflated. Irritated with myself for thinking . . . What? That she cares about me? Grow up, Will.

'What happened – with Yan. You were there, weren't you?'

'Kind of. I didn't really see . . .' I look down. Don't give anything away. Trouble is, Claire's the sort you want to confide in. She makes you feel a better person for letting things out, saying how you feel. She's clever like that – she wheedles stuff out of you, then pounces when she hears what she's known all along you were thinking. She'd be a great interrogator. People would be queuing up to tell her stuff.

'Right.' She looks disappointed. She looks as though she doesn't believe me. I feel disappointed too, but I can't put my finger on why.

'So how's it going? Otherwise, I mean.'

Crap question. Stupid question. But what else do you say?

'Good,' she says. 'I mean, you know, fine.'

I nod. She nods. It's one of those awkward silences. I hate them – I usually just walk away. I'm tempted to do that right now, but I don't. That's the thing with

Claire. You can't walk away. I can't, I mean.

'You're not eating,' she says.

'Not hungry,' I lie. Although I do seem to have lost my appetite a bit.

She nods again. 'You want to go for a walk?'

I get a funny feeling in my stomach. Surprise maybe?

'Sure.' I wait for her to stand up first, just in case. In case of what? Who knows. She does stand up, though, and I follow her out of the canteen. I feel self-conscious, too big all of a sudden. I've always been taller than her but in the last two years I've grown even more. When we're in the courtyard outside the canteen, she slows down a bit and I catch up so we're walking side by side. My heart's beating rapidly and my palms are sweating. I tell myself to calm down. I tell myself this is no big deal.

'So what happened in History?'

We're out of earshot of anyone; now I know why Claire wanted to go for a walk. Again I get a slight surge of disappointment, but not as much this time. She's interested in me at least.

'I dunno.' I put my hands in my pockets. I feel stupid. I want to tell her, want to admit that I really don't know, that I lost it, that it was terrifying, that the pain was so unbearable I didn't know what to do with myself, that I could hear voices in my head, see things that I recognised but couldn't place, feel things that I didn't understand. Like fear, hatred, anger. I want to tell Claire that I'm afraid I'm going

84

mad. I want to ask her for help.

But it's not going to happen. I mean, why would she want to help me? Part of the reason I don't talk to anyone, don't hang out with anyone, is because of what I know about myself. I mean, the truth is, why would anyone want to hang out with me? Claire obviously doesn't – otherwise we wouldn't have been virtual strangers for two years. It's bad enough hanging out with myself; I wouldn't want to impose it on others.

'That's it? You don't know?'

She's looking at me intently, those eyes of hers boring into mine. She doesn't let you get away with anything, Claire.

'I just . . .' I look away awkwardly. 'Look, let's drop it, OK?'

She always used to tell me I was evasive. I realise no one's told me that for a long time; it occurs to me that maybe no one's cared enough to notice.

'I don't mean to be evasive,' I say, to make her realise I know what she's thinking, to remind her of what she used to say to me, to tell her I haven't forgotten.

She rolls her eyes. 'Well, you are,' she says, but there's a little smile playing on her lips. 'For the record, you did look awful. Really ill. Mrs Draper should have realised.'

'Yeah, well.' I manage half a smile too. You'd have to look hard to see it, but it's there.

Another pause, then, 'How's your dad?' I look at

her in mock surprise. Claire and my dad don't get on. He doesn't like her family and he doesn't like her. She's never been anything but polite about him but I know she thinks he's an idiot, a right-wing ignoramus. She's wrong. He's not an ignoramus.

'He's working on Yan's case, isn't he? He's going to be the prosecutor, I mean.'

Back to Yan again. I'm silent for a few seconds. 'Yeah. Yeah, he is,' I say moodily. 'He thinks Yan did it. Other than that, he's fine.'

'He thinks he did it? Based on what? Based on what evidence?' Her voice has gone about an octave higher; her hands are in fists. All because of Yan? What's the big deal?

'I guess the fact that he was there. Holding the knife,' I say.

'He took the knife out, Will. He's terrified. He went to help Mr Best and now he's being accused of murder. But he didn't do it. Why would he? You know Yan. You know he wouldn't hurt a fly. I'm really scared for him, Will.'

I'm feeling uncomfortable; I want to change the subject. I remember being in Yan's garden, years ago, remember him coming across a baby bird, still half in its egg, on the ground. It had fallen out of the tree, Yan said. I remember the way he tended to it, taking it inside, keeping it warm, feeding it milk. Remember how devastated he was when it died anyway.

But that was a long time ago. People change. Everything changes.

I push the image from my head.

'How are your parents?'

Claire's cheeks are slightly flushed; she looks at me warily. 'They're fine,' she says. 'Mum had to have an operation last month but she's much better now.'

'Good. That's good.'

We drift into silence again. We're near the school gates – time to turn back, to walk along the fence, back around the netball and baseball courts. I stop. I can see him outside the gates. A man. He's looking at me. He's one of them, I know it; I can see it in his eyes. Pain, hope, a recognition. I feel my stomach clench with fear.

I look back at Claire; her face is pointed in concentration. Maybe she's trying to think of something to say. Maybe there *is* nothing else to say.

The man is still there, hunched slightly, standing on the other side of the road looking right at me. You'd think someone would have arrested him or something, hanging outside a school like that. He looks dodgy. Looks like a freak.

I glance at Claire furtively. 'You see that man?'

She frowns as though I've startled her slightly. 'What man?'

'There.' I point; she looks over.

'Sure. What about him?'

'You think he looks weird?'

Her frown deepens. 'Weird? Not really.'

'What's he doing there, though?' I ask. 'I mean, he's just standing there staring at us.'

'He's not staring at us; he's looking into the middle distance,' Claire says. 'And I imagine what he's doing there is waiting for the bus.'

I do a double take. I hadn't seen the bus stop. I feel stupid.

'I've got a class,' Claire says. 'You coming in?'

I look back at the man. He's looking at me reproachfully, like I shouldn't have said anything. It makes me angry; there is no secret between us, nothing that I should protect. He is nothing to do with me. I'll do what I want, tell who I want.

'He's still looking,' I say.

Claire shakes her head. 'You still think people are following you, don't you?' She says it sympathetically. 'Come on. Let's head back.'

She's a few feet away from me; I could walk with her, back into school, back into normality.

'I can't,' I say. 'I have to go.'

'Where?' she asks. Always direct; Claire doesn't have any truck with subtlety, with dancing around a subject tentatively.

'I just . . .' I look back at the man, then I turn to her. 'I'll see you later, OK?'

'Sure,' she says. She looks vaguely dissatisfied; she opens her mouth to speak, then closes it again. She walks away. I turn and start to walk quickly towards the school gates. I want to know if she's watching me, but I can't look back. It would tell her too much.

*   *   *

88

It started with trees. Yan's dad said he was going to plant some. He had an idea for a semicircle of them at the bottom of his garden. Said it would create symmetry with the semicircle patio at the top of their garden. He told Mum and Dad about it when we were in our garden one day. Mum had invited them round. She'd argued with Dad about it; told him that she wasn't succumbing to the 'hideous prejudice that seems to have built up around here'. I remember wondering what prejudice was.

Anyway, they were all drinking beer; Yan's mum wasn't there because she was cooking something for us at home, but Yan and his brother were in our garden kicking a football about; Claire and I were watching them and pretending we found the adults' conversation utterly boring. Her parents were at a conference; she was spending the day with us until they picked her up much later.

Mum went inside and brought us some lemonade. It was a really hot day; we glugged it down and fell down on our backs on the grass. One of those hot summer days when you don't want to go inside, not even when it starts to get dark.

My parents and Yan's dad sat there all afternoon; then, at some point, must have been early evening, Yan's mum appeared with all this food. It was hot and spicy and I remember seeing Dad looking at Mum uncertainly, but she just gave him one of her looks, and I saw it and made sure she didn't see me look uncertain, even though spicy food wasn't exactly what I had in mind on a hot balmy evening either.

She was right to shoot us a look, of course; the food was incredible. Warmed you up on the inside and cooled you down on the outside. Not that Dad would have known that; he barely touched it, instead just sat silently and regarded it with suspicion. But Mum and I did. We started tentatively, then we fell upon it and Yan's mum looked all pleased and proud as it was all devoured in front of her. She said next time she'd make more and Mum moaned and said she couldn't because she'd have to eat it and her stomach was already stretched beyond capacity. Yan's mum started to clear everything up, but Mum wouldn't let her; she pulled out a chair and poured her some lemonade and told her to stay. And Yan's mum protested a little bit but my mum didn't take no for an answer, so she stayed, and we all just sat there, watching the sky slowly get darker, listening to the crickets chirruping, thinking to ourselves that things didn't get much better than this.

And that's when Yan's dad mentioned the trees. He said he'd been looking into it and he was going to buy some conifers. Small ones. He was going to watch them grow. He said that British people grew British trees and he smiled to himself and said that the trees would be like his family; they would put down roots and grow big and strong.

I remember noticing my mum and dad exchange glances and I got that feeling when you know something's going on that you can't see or understand yet.

'Conifers?' my mum said, with a little smile. 'You know they grow very fast. And very tall.'

Yan's dad grinned. 'Exactly,' he said, rubbing his hands together.

'They'd better not grow too fast,' my dad said. 'Don't want a whole bunch of them blocking out our sun, do we?'

Yan's dad laughed. 'We shall see how big they grow, shall we? You could plant some too. We could have a race.' He opened another beer. 'Conifers,' he said. 'I think they sound like very good trees. Very good trees indeed.'

Claire's gone, disappeared through the school's main door. She'll be in a classroom now, getting out her books. Organised, punctual, responsible, that's Claire. I wonder briefly what she thinks of me, then I decide I probably don't want to know. I'm still at the school gate, looking at the man at the bus stop.

Slowly, as though I'm being pulled by a magnet, I walk towards the school gates. I cross the road. The man is still there, still looking at me; he knows I'm walking directly towards him but he doesn't move, doesn't look away.

I keep walking; I'm inches away from him now. Then I stop.

'Leave me alone.' I say it in a deep, low voice for maximum impact. 'I don't know who you are but I know you're one of the freaks. I'm not interested in you or your weird cult. Just leave. Now.'

He looks even more tired close up. Not tired like he hasn't slept; it's more than that, like the weight of the world is pressing down on his shoulders. It's oppressive. I feel like if I look at him too long I'll be sucked in, that I'll be carrying the weight too. It scares me.

'You don't know who you are.' He says it sadly, reproachfully.

'Yes, I do,' I say firmly. 'I know exactly who I am. You don't. You know nothing about me. Which is why you have to leave. Otherwise I'm going to call someone. The police. Social services.' I'm puffing out my chest slightly but I know I'm not kidding anyone.

'You know who you are now, perhaps, but that isn't who you really are,' the man says, moving his hand to my shoulder; I shake it off, but it doesn't throw him off his stride. 'I don't understand what has happened, but you must remember,' he implores me. 'You must listen to us. You are one of us.' He says it again. 'You are one of us.'

One of us. Part of something. I am part of something. I feel myself drawn in. My brethren. My friends. Then I shake myself. I am repulsed by my weakness. I'm not part of anything. They are *freaks*.

'I am *not* one of you.' I pull back. All pretence at bravery has gone; I want to run now, want to have someone there I can stand behind, someone who can defend me.

'You are one of us,' he repeats like a scratched CD. 'You are a Returner.'

My fear subsides briefly, overtaken by irritation. Irritation and anger. 'I am not a "Returner",' I say levelly. 'There is no such thing. I've done research. You're just some loons, that's all.'

'You are a Returner. You have lived with us through history. You remember. Like us, you remember.' He's getting quite agitated now, waving his hands like a total weirdo. I look around to check no one's watching us.

'I remember? Yeah, well, that's the fundamental problem in your little theory, isn't it?' Sarcasm. Now I'm on safer ground. 'Because I *don't* remember. I don't remember you, or anything about being a Returner. Which would suggest that you've got the wrong person, wouldn't it? I mean, logically, you're not exactly on firm ground, are you?'

I'm feeling good, feeling on top of things. It doesn't last.

'You will remember. And we will be there for you when you do,' the man says. 'You are one of us. We are worried for you. Don't be afraid. This is your destiny.'

I'm looking at him, into his eyes, which is a mistake. I remember my dreams. I feel cold suddenly.

'Yeah, well, that's something else I don't buy,' I say uncomfortably. 'Destiny. It's a load of rubbish. There's no such thing.'

'Not yet, perhaps.' He turns and gets on to a bus

that has stopped. I didn't notice it arrive. 'Remember, we're here. When you need us.'

'I won't need you,' I say, but I don't think he hears me.

CHAPTER NINE

I get home in a filthy mood. I'm angry at Yan. Every time I close my eyes I can see him, see those dark soulful eyes of his, looking at me reproachfully. Because I didn't help. Because he's in prison and I'm not. Because Dad's right, he should never have come here in the first place. Because of the way Claire looks when she talks about him. Because Patrick didn't listen properly. Because . . . Because . . . Because this is all his fault. And even if it isn't, it doesn't matter, I'm still angry with him. And at everyone else too. My brain feels like a fog has descended. I want the freaks to leave me alone. I want to feel normal, want to have conversations with Claire and go to school and be like everyone else.

Claire. Claire and Yan.

No. There's no 'Claire and Yan'. Claire's just concerned for him. She's like that. She worries about people.

I push the door open; I can tell Dad is home because it's on the latch. You'd think he'd be more security conscious; he makes out like there are immigrants on every street corner ready to steal the shirt off your back. I think it's because he can't be bothered getting up if anyone calls round. This way they just come right in. This way he doesn't have to move anywhere.

He's in the kitchen. I hear the clink of his glass as he puts it down on the table. There are voices; he's not alone.

'That you, son?'

'Yeah.'

'Just finishing up some business here. You all right?'

'Fine.'

He doesn't want me in the kitchen. We understand each other, Dad and I; understand what meaning we imbue words with. 'You all right?' doesn't mean, 'Are you all right?'; it means, 'Are you OK leaving us alone for a while? Can you not bother us, please?'

Actually, there's rarely a 'please' attached.

It means I can't get anything to eat so I head for the sitting room which adjoins the kitchen and decide to wait it out. I flick on the television. Nothing's on. I'm about to turn it off when I hear the name 'Yan'. It's Patrick. I sit down silently on a chair. The TV is on loud enough for them to think I can't hear, but I can.

'They bloody rejected it. I thought you were in control. I thought you could handle it.'

'And I thought you said it was done and dusted,' Dad replies. 'When it isn't. There are holes everywhere.' He sounds tense. A moment later the door to the sitting room opens and his head pops round it, I think to check that I'm not listening to them. I look straight ahead at the television.

'What is it?' I ask, as if surprised to see him.

'Nothing, son. You all right?'

'I'm fine.'

'All right then.'

He shuts the door behind him, more tightly this time. I turn the TV down.

'It's the forensics team that's the problem,' Dad says. 'They say the knife went in at a strange angle.'

'A strange angle? Who cares about the angle? The boy was found with the knife. He was found standing over the body with the knife.'

'The forensics report corroborates his story. I thought you said you had the police. I thought you said it was sorted.'

Patrick clears his throat. 'Must be a bloody cock-up somewhere. In the meantime, we need to do something about it.'

'I'm all ears.' Dad's voice sounds strangled. 'Because from where I'm sitting this looks like a bloody disaster. Are we doing the right thing here? Are you sure this is going to work?'

'Work? Of course it will.' Patrick sounds angry suddenly. 'It has to work. Have you forgotten what happened to you? Have you forgotten what people like him have done to you? Have you forgotten Chloe?'

There's a long silence. My hair is on end. Chloe. Mum. Why would anyone have forgotten her? What's she got to do with anything anyway?

'I'll never forget Chloe,' Dad says then. He sounds choked up.

'Of course you won't. But things need doing. Don't they? Don't they?'

There's another silence, shorter this time.

'Don't you worry,' Patrick says then, his voice soothing. 'Boy's going to get his comeuppance. You've been waiting for this a long time.'

'A very long time,' Dad says.

'And after this other people will realise what's going on too. This is the beginning. People have to feel the fear to make them remember their desire for a safer country, a country that belongs to us again.'

'To us,' Dad says, his voice a bit more level.

'Just think,' Patrick continues, 'next year there's an election. Next year things could finally change. You want that, don't you? Don't you? You can get people onside. People like you. You're important to us. You know that, don't you?'

'Yeah. I suppose.'

'And we're here for you. The National Party is on your side. We want what's ours to stay ours. Stop these filthy thieves in their tracks. That's what that man is. A filthy thief. He stole from you. He stole plain and simple. And now you're going to get your revenge. You want that. I know you do.'

'Yes. Yes, I do.'

'So then, you know what we have to do.'

'Yes. And I'll do it. I'll do what I can.'

A chair moves slightly. 'You'll do more than that.' Patrick's voice drops; I lower the volume of the television. 'You just remember that without me you're nothing, OK? No job, no money, nothing. You owe me. I ask you to jump, you say, 'How high?' Right? Right?'

'I'll do whatever needs to be done,' Dad corrects himself. 'I didn't mean anything by that. I meant . . . I'll do it, Patrick. You can count on me. Only . . .'

'Only what?'

'Will. You can't use him? Instead, I mean?'

'Unreliable witness,' Patrick says. 'The boy's confused about what he saw. Defence would wipe the floor with him. You know that.'

'So tell me again what's going to happen.'

'It's nothing,' Patrick says. 'I'll just see to it that the house is searched again. On a technicality. And this time we're going to find something. Another knife. Shows intent.'

'And where are you going to find it?'

There's a pause. 'We haven't decided yet. Needs to be somewhere we wouldn't have found it before, obviously. But until we're there . . . Floorboards, possibly. That's always a good one. Up the chimney.'

'You wouldn't have looked up the chimney the first time you searched?'

'Floorboards then.' Patrick sounds irritable. 'Leave that to me. You just expect new evidence tomorrow, and make sure it tips the scales. OK? I'm depending on you. We all are.'

'I'll be on it,' Dad says.

'Good. We can't afford any more mistakes.'

'No.'

The glass comes down on the table. A chair scrapes back. 'You're doing the right thing, trust me,' Patrick says.

They're walking out of the kitchen. I quickly turn the television up, move closer to it, try to look like I've been watching. I feel fake. How does someone look like they've been watching television and not eavesdropping? As they walk past the door, Patrick looks in.

'Watching telly? What about homework?' He's smiling; his expression looks forced.

I shrug. 'I'll do it later.'

'Later? That's the trouble with this generation.' He turns to Dad, who's coming up behind him. 'Do it later, pay for it later, worry about it later. What about the here and now, eh? Eh?'

'Why do now what you can put off until tomorrow,' Dad says darkly.

He's kind of smiling, but I know he isn't joking. He's got this look in his eye that I recognise, that makes me shrink back. Best to lie low. That way he's less likely to lose it. That's what happens sometimes. He says he doesn't mean to. He's always really sorry afterwards. But his anger just gets the better of him, he says. And then the next day I have to wear long sleeves, keep my face covered, tell people I fell off my bike, even though I never ride it any more.

They say goodbye; Dad closes the door. He takes it off the latch – no more visitors tonight.

He walks in and sits on the sofa. I look at him; I want to ask him about Mum, about what she's got to do with Yan, with his dad. I want to ask him about the knife too. I want him to say something that reassures me I got the completely wrong idea from their conversation. But I don't. I don't want to risk it.

He leans back and puts his feet up. His face looks strained. 'What are we watching?'

I look at the television, startled. I have no idea what is on; I haven't actually been focusing on the screen.

'Nothing,' I say.

He seems satisfied. 'You won't mind if I put the History Channel on then?'

'Sure.' I throw him the remote control. He catches it. He might be getting on, but his reflexes are still good. He used to be a sportsman; he taught me how to play football, how to play cricket. We'd stay out in the garden for hours on summer evenings, kicking or batting balls to each other.

It stopped after Mum died. A lot of things stopped then.

There's a black and white film on with soldiers marching. 'Was that about Yan?' I can't help it; I have to ask.

He doesn't look at me.

'Can't talk about work, you know that,' he says.

'Did he do it, though? Do they know for sure yet?'

'Looks that way.'

He's staring at the television. He's uncomfortable. I don't know if that makes me feel better or worse. I know what I heard and I know that Dad is refusing to catch my eye.

'They're scum. All of them,' he says. He sounds angry, but when I look at his face I think I can see tears in his eyes.

I look away, embarrassed. And then I get a flash. Yan in prison. No more Claire walking along the river with him. He'd be out of the way.

I can't believe I thought that.

There's no Claire and Yan anyway.

I shake myself. I'm feeling hot. I need a drink.

'I'm getting a drink. Want anything?'

Dad holds up his glass. It's still half full. 'No, I'm all right.'

I go into the kitchen, turn on the tap and pour myself a glass of water, downing it in one, feeling its coolness spreading out through my stomach.

Maybe Yan *did* do it. If someone else had done it, the police would have caught them. *Don't ask questions. Don't analyse. Just follow the path ahead.* Yes. Yes, exactly. The voice in my head makes sense. Don't analyse. That's Claire's problem – she worries too much. Yan's just another one of her causes – like the donkeys. I'd forgotten about the donkeys. She found out that they got beaten sometimes – the ones on the beaches where they walk them up and down all day – and decided she was going to start her own donkey sanctuary. She hates cruelty, Claire. She'd adopt half the world if she could.

But you can't, can you? You just have to get on with it. Keep your head down and only look up if you have to.

'There's some pie in the oven,' Dad calls out. 'Help yourself. You could put some chips on too.'

I don't feel hungry. 'Maybe later.'

'Suit yourself.'

I hesitate by the door.

'If he did it, will he go to prison for a long time?' I'm leaning against the door frame tentatively.

Dad's face turns towards me. I think he's smiling. 'We can only hope.'

I'm not moving. I bite my lip awkwardly.

'Son,' Dad says, looking at me carefully, 'is there something on your mind?'

I take a breath. 'No . . . I just, you know, want to know.'

'I know.' He puts his drink down. 'I know you used to like him. But people turn bad, Will. People are bad. His family . . . They're bad news. We've known that for years. You move to a country, you have to respect it, respect its people, its traditions. You have to see where you fit in. His family are like the rest of them. Foreigners are never interested in fitting in, just in taking over. And now look what's happened. He has to pay for what he's done, Will. People always have to pay.'

I don't go to bed until late, too late, and even then I can't sleep. I lie there thinking, not about anything properly – my brain is like a scattergun, full of thoughts and images but none of them are related, none of them go anywhere. It's all just random, all just flashing up.

Maybe that's the point. Maybe everything is random.

I want my mind to slow down. I count to a hundred and then count back down to one. By the time I'm in the seventies my mind is wandering again, but less like a slide show, more like the wandering it does before you fall asleep. Semi-conscious. Calm.

Sixty-three's the last number I remember counting.

Then I'm not counting any more.

The cold is not just around me; it is part of me. My clothes are no protection; my hands and feet are blocks of ice, crying out for mercy. On we trudge. The man in front of me is stumbling; his coat is torn, his boots too big. Not his. He hobbles. He has grey hair; he is too old for this place. A mistake, perhaps. He turns, catches my eye briefly, then immediately turns back again. He seems disoriented. The cold can do that to you. I think I recognise him. He used to own a shop in the village where I grew up. He was always kind, always had a joke with us. Suddenly he falls sideways, into the snow, the ice. He rolls over; his eyes are wide with terror. He pulls himself up. 'Comrade,' he says, although it is barely a word. 'Comrade, if you would just . . . I can still . . . A stone – I tripped over a stone.' His voice is rasping; he scrabbles desperately. I watch as a bayonet lands on his head; it kills him immediately, his blood unspeakably bright against the white beneath him. A voice: 'Comrade? He is no comrade. He is useless. You see what happens, if you don't pull your weight? Learn from this. And keep walking.' I start to walk again. I do not look back.

A new place. It is dusty. No, not dust. Ash. It sticks in my throat and my nose. It permeates everything. I want to leave here. It is a bad place. I watch the line, the pathetic line, weaving its way towards the doors, human but only just – not enough flesh to be fully human. Children clutching hands, men with hollow eyes, others with grit – they will not give up, not until they have to. The line moves and I move too. An ending, a beginning, I don't know any more. This place is not what I expected. I breathe; the ash is choking me. I know where it comes from. I know. I walk forward. I look at no one . . .

And now another place, more familiar but I can't place it. There are lorries, people being herded on to them. Like sheep. We are all sheep. It is for improvement. Flaws eradicated, evolution once more on track. The inside of the lorry is dark. People are screaming, they fear the lorries, they run, they are chased. Gunfire, then more screaming. Resistance is futile. Some give up. Others urge people not to make a fuss, not to cause more problems. I feel bodies pushing against me as more people are forced into the lorries. There are no lines, there is little organisation. A voice is shouting, 'Britain for Britons. Britain for Britons.' Someone shouts, 'Bigots! You can't do this!' There is a loud bang. I feel something fall against me; it is a woman. She has long hair. She looks at me as she falls, her eyes wide in shock. She is bleeding. She clutches at my shoulders. 'This must end.' She is sinking down to the floor. I can't help her. I am hot. I am sweating. I am screaming. No. No! NO!

I open my eyes. My bed is drenched in sweat. Did I shout out? I listen tentatively for Dad to come in, to see what's going on; he doesn't. I am panting, out of breath. It was a dream. Just a dream.

I get out of bed. It was just a dream, I tell myself again, more firmly this time.

I'm trembling. I realise I'm cold. I pull on some clothes. I don't want to get back into bed. I need to get out of this room; I feel like I'm suffocating.

My eyes are drawn to the window. I pull back the curtains. I can see Claire's room. The lights are off; she's asleep. I look at my watch: 2.46 a.m. I look back at Claire's room. Ten minutes pass. Without thinking too much about what I'm doing, I carefully open the window, doing my best to stop it squeaking too much. Then I hang my legs out of it, turn around so I'm holding on to the windowsill by my hands and drop down. The grass is wet beneath my feet. I look back up to make sure no one's heard me then laugh at myself. Dad will have drunk too much whisky to hear anything.

I run down to the end of the garden and pull myself over the fence. Now I'm padding up Claire's garden. I reach her house; I'm underneath her window. I stop. What am I doing? This is crazy. I'm going to go home. I don't know what I was thinking.

I start to move, then stop. I bring my hands to my mouth and coo like a pigeon. It's what we used to do. It was our call.

I wait a few seconds; she hasn't heard me. Or she's ignoring me. If I go now, I can pretend it never happened. I start to jog back towards the fence. Then I hear something. I stop. I turn around. Claire's window is open. She is looking at me strangely, her face pale in the moonlight. She looks like Rapunzel, like I could climb up her hair.

'Will? Is that you?' She sounds incredulous but not surprised. 'Do you know what time it is?'

CHAPTER TEN

I don't know why I'm here, can't remember what propelled me out of the window. I'm embarrassed; I'm nervous. I have climbed up into Claire's bedroom and she has given me a glass of water; I'm sitting at the end of her bed. She is looking at me expectantly. It's nearly 3 a.m. and I have pitched up, cooing like a pigeon for the first time in years. I can't believe she let me in, if I'm honest.

'I should go,' is all I can think of to say. What does she think of me? I don't want to care, but I do. Desperately. Which is why I want to leave. I need her approval too much. It makes me feel vulnerable.

Claire rolls her eyes. 'You came all this way to say that?'

I scowl. Her voice isn't as soft as I'd like. Her eyes aren't as forgiving.

'I thought . . .' I look down. I don't want to leave,

not really. 'I don't know what I thought. I just . . .'

'Will, you're as white as a sheet and you're shaking. Just sit there for a little while if you want. Then you can tell me what the matter is. OK?'

It sounds reasonable enough. I nod. I like hearing her say my name.

'So?' Claire asks.

I get the feeling my little while is up. I shrug. 'I guess I had a nightmare, that's all.'

'You still get those?'

I look at her sharply. 'I got them before?'

'You've always had them. Ever since I've known you.'

'Right.' I feel unsettled. I'd forgotten I'd had them so long. I'd sort of thought it had been a year, two years tops.

'So what was your nightmare about?'

I feel stupid suddenly. It was just a dream. It's not important or anything.

'I dunno. People dying.'

'Which people?' She isn't looking at me like I'm crazy. She seems interested.

'People. First on a ship. I think it was a ship. Then . . .' I trail off. If it was someone else I'd think they were only getting me to talk so they could laugh at me later. Claire, though, she's not like that. I wish I could be more like her sometimes.

She's looking at me intently, encouraging me to go on. 'You're here. You got out of bed and came here. So you might as well tell me,' she says, as though she can hear my thoughts.

I tell her. I describe the dreams in all their detail – and I find I can remember way more than I thought I could. As I talk I feel the hairs on my arms standing upright and the fear returning. No, not fear. It's like fear but different. It's more like dread. I shiver.

She's frowning, nodding her head every so often. Active listening, they call it. I learnt that phrase from my therapist. He said Dad and I should listen to each other more. He told Dad that listening didn't mean just sitting there; it meant taking an active interest, nodding, saying things like, 'That must be hard for you,' or, 'And how does that make you feel?' That was when I realised that the shrink was doing it too; that he wasn't really interested, he was just pretending to be interested by saying the right things. Active listening. Phoney listening. I stopped going to him after that.

But Claire isn't nodding and saying things because she learnt how to do it. She's doing it genuinely. I feel a sudden burst of love for her, a huge surge of emotion that threatens to take hold of me, make me grab her or do something else crazy. I swallow. I box it as quickly as I can, push the emotion away.

I tell her about the least scary dreams first; I want to ease her in gradually. I describe a dream where I was in a ship. I felt seasick. There were too many men down there with me.

'A ship?' she asks seriously. 'You were at the bottom of it?' she asks. I nod. 'Describe it,' she says. 'As best you can.'

I describe what it was like. I describe the smell, the atmosphere of fear and desperation. I describe the walls of wood, the deafening sound of the waves crashing against them, the feeling of claustrophobia, the knowledge that for good or ill we were all in this together, that we would all sink or swim together.

'Right . . . OK. Wait there.' She gets off the bed and moves over to her computer, turning it on and staring at it seriously. She starts to type something, then she turns back to me.

'Tell me about the next dream.'

I take a deep breath. Then I start talking. About the comrades, the strange bitter chocolate, about the lines of people. And somehow I don't stop. It's 5 a.m. by the time I've finished. I feel exhausted, as though I've run a marathon or something. But the release . . . it's incredible, like gasping for air when you've been drowning. I don't show it, of course. I do nothing. I box the feelings, hide them.

Claire's still clacking away at her computer. I lean back on her bed and close my eyes. It's warm here. Cosy. Safe. There's something about girls' rooms – the smell of creams and sweet things, the layers of things. Like not just a duvet, but a duvet and a sheet and a blanket and a throw and cushions and a teddy bear. Girls get away with having teddy bears when they're way too old for them. No one thinks they're pathetic. Even the lighting's good – she's got a little lamp and she's draped a scarf over it so it emits this low-level pinky sort of light that makes you feel as if you're in a womb or something. How do girls think of things like putting scarves over lamps?

'OK.'

I open my eyes slowly. I must have drifted off. 'OK what?' I pull myself up; I'm sheepish suddenly – I've been sleeping on Claire's bed. I've still got my shoes on and I can see I've left traces of grass and mud on her yellow checked blanket.

'OK, I know what these dreams are,' she says. She looks excited, like she's solved a puzzle. Triumphant, in fact.

I raise an eyebrow. 'You do?'

'Yes!' she says, grinning now. 'So the first one: you were dreaming you were on a slave ship. Look!' She pulls an image of a ship and my eyes widen in recognition. 'This was the sort of ship they transported slaves in. From Africa to the Caribbean. It's exactly as you described it.'

I stare at the screen uncertainly as she scrolls down. 'I dreamt about slaves?'

'We studied them, remember? About three years ago? You never seemed to be paying attention but you must have been.'

I don't remember studying slaves. Mind you, I don't remember a lot of things. Dad calls it selective memory; he says I only remember what I want to.

'And the others?' I ask. I feel as though someone's opened a door, like I've been in prison and suddenly realised there's a way out. It's just History lessons giving me nightmares. I've always hated History lessons and now I know why. It's not because I'm stupid or lazy; it's because they mess with my head. They're to blame for everything.

Claire claps her hands. 'It's all history. You described the decimation of a Native American settlement. Look, there's a first-person account here, a letter written by a white man who befriended the Indians, and it virtually describes everything you said.'

'We studied Native Americans?' I ask. I want to believe her, want to buy into this theory.

'Well, no, but we studied the other things . . .' Claire's forehead wrinkles. 'You must have seen the Native Americans somewhere. Television maybe.'

I nod uncertainly.

'Next?'

She looks down. 'I think . . .' She bites her lip. 'I think the one with the line of people, the smoke . . .'

I look down. I don't want to remember it. I'm feeling very strange. I'm not feeling warm and cosy any more; I'm feeling as if the walls are pressing in on me.

'I think it might have been . . . I mean, I'm not sure, but I think you were dreaming about the concentration camps. The Nazi ones. The ones we're doing now.'

'So basically I'm a historical genius?' I force a little laugh, but already I'm getting a funny feeling in the pit of my stomach. Sick again. I know now that the headache will follow. I want to clutch my stomach as it spasms but I don't want to look like a weirdo.

'I don't know about genius, but it makes sense, you have to admit,' Claire says.

'I'd better go. It's late.' I'm trying to sound normal, trying not to let my discomfort show. If I'm going to freak out, I don't want to do it here.

'It's early, you mean. Don't go. We're getting somewhere.' There's the faint trace of a smile on Claire's lips. It makes me feel a bit better. Maybe I can stay. Maybe I'm not going to freak out after all. I take a deep breath. The spasms are slowing. I can control this. I have to. I don't want to go, not yet.

'So what about the last dream?' I say. 'Come on then, which lesson is that based on?'

'I don't know.' She frowns. 'But we'll find out.'

'Maybe,' I say, sounding more sarcastic than I'd intended. It's disappointment really. I want everything sewn up neatly; don't want any unanswered questions hanging around.

'Definitely,' Claire says. 'Anyway, the point is, your dreams aren't anything to worry about. You're just reliving History lessons.'

'History lessons I don't remember,' I say.

I don't know why I'm being obnoxious. Actually, I do. It's what I do. A defence mechanism, my shrink would have called it. Probably. I realise I'm staring at Claire. I realise she's staring back at me. I go red. I'm hot. I don't want to look away. I don't ever want to look away.

She smiles uncertainly. 'So they went into your subconscious mind instead of your conscious one,' she says. 'Just go to sleep when you do your GCSE and you'll get an A.'

I find myself laughing. Then she's laughing too.

'There I was, thinking I was deep,' I say with a little grin. 'Guess I'm not after all.'

'Guess not,' Claire deadpans. She's still looking at me. Is there tension in the air or is it just me? If I was someone else, if we were somewhere else, I'd kiss her. I'd grab her, like they do in films, and I'd kiss her. Or maybe I'd just bury my head in her shoulder and pull her really tight, feel her heart beating through my skin.

No, I'd definitely kiss her.

Does she want me to? Should I?

She's going to say something. What? I move closer. My skin feels all prickly.

Her expression is intense. 'Will?'

I nod in response. I don't trust myself to speak.

'Is your dad any further on Yan's case?'

A hit to the stomach. A moment of readjustment. I recoil inside. I can't let her see my disappointment. Yan. Of course. 'I dunno.' It's a meaningless answer, but it's all I can come up with.

'My parents think they're going to try and pin it on him. Because Patrick . . .' She looks at me warily. 'Because your dad's friend wants to make a political point.'

'Yeah?' I try to sound uninterested, hoping she'll change the subject.

'The Nationalist Party. It's trying to get support for

the deportation of immigrants by making out they're all criminals and on benefits, which is patently ridiculous. I mean Yan's father owns a big company.'

'Which laid off five hundred people last month,' I say. She was the one who brought it up. If she wants to talk about Yan and his father, that's fine by me. Absolutely fine.

'Like every other company, Will. We're in a recession, remember?'

She's got fire in her eyes; I shrug. Always so political, Claire.

'Look, the police know what they're doing,' I say. I want her to look at me again with that intensity. Or was I imagining it?

'Maybe they do. But that doesn't mean they're doing the right thing. Did you know that in prisons the ratio of British nationals of foreign descent to white British has increased twenty-fold in the last few years? And that attack on the steelworkers – it was driven by the sort of propaganda that the Nationalist Party have been churning out. Like it's them against us. But it isn't. We're all in this together. We're all just people, Will. And now Yan's in prison for something he didn't do. It's terrifying, don't you think?'

I look at her irritably. The intensity isn't going to come back. She never wanted me to kiss her. And now we're talking about Yan. How does he manage to work his way into everything even when he's banged up?

'I don't really know,' I say.

'You don't know?' She's agitated now; I regret even responding. 'You know that any first-generation immigrant is now deported as a matter of course as soon as they leave prison? That they can't come back, ever? That's why the prisons are filling up with immigrants. It's deportation by the back door. Mum says it's a huge conspiracy. She says the Nationalist Party is behind it. They want to get rid of anyone who isn't white. The chief of police is a member.'

Her eyes are boring into me; I can't look at them.

Her eyes, imploring. She won't look away. She holds up her baby. The ice is melting and I can't stop it. Cracks are appearing. No. I mustn't look at her. But she is too compelling. I can't look away . . .

I shake myself. I don't care about whatever it is Claire's blathering on about. It's nothing to do with me. What happens to Yan, to all these people, is nothing to do with her either.

'Look, I should get going,' I say, more determinedly this time.

'That's it? That's all you've got to say?'

God, she's hard work. I'd forgotten about that. I get up and walk towards the door, then I realise if I'm going to get out of her room unnoticed by her parents I've got to go the way I came in. I walk back towards the bed. Claire's staring at me. Her clear, honest eyes, looking right into mine. Eyes that make me want to be better than I am. Eyes that make me feel like I *can* be better.

'For what it's worth, I don't think he did it,'

I mutter. 'Yan, I mean.' It's a moment of weakness. I regret it almost as soon as the words have left my mouth.

'Of course he didn't,' Claire says vehemently. Then her eyes narrow. 'Why? Why don't you think he did it?'

I ignore my inner voice, which is shouting at me to keep my mouth shut, not to get involved. 'It looked to me like he was trying to help Mr Best. Like he was trying to give him mouth-to-mouth.'

'I knew it!' Her eyes light up and just seeing them makes me feel like she's flicked a switch inside me too. I realise I told her what I saw specifically to get this reaction, her approval. I feel like I'm walking on air all of a sudden, even though I know I'm going to fall soon enough.

'You've told your Dad?' she asks.

I nod. No need to tell her he didn't listen to me. She's smiling and that's all that matters. I can see the sun beginning to rise through her curtains.

I jump up on the bed. I have to get away. From her eyes. From her.

'It was good to see you, Will,' Claire says quietly. 'I'm always here. You know, if you want to talk . . .'

I nod matter-of-factly. Elation boxed. Lid down firmly.

I open the window. The fresh air feels invigorating. I climb out, turning so I can shimmy down to the garden. I hesitate.

'Thanks,' I say. 'Thanks a lot.'

CHAPTER ELEVEN

By the time I get back to my own bed it's time to get up again. It actually feels as though I've been asleep anyway; I was at Claire's for nearly three hours but now it all feels like a dream. A nice dream. I haven't had a dream like that in a very long time. Haven't felt that warm, that . . . happy.

History lessons. The History Channel. Didn't Mum always say too much television would give me nightmares? I don't know why it's such a relief. But it is. One thing explained, one thing less freaky. There'll be some explanation for the weirdos who follow me too, I know there will. Maybe they're a well-known cult I just haven't heard of. Maybe I'll mention them to Claire again, see if she can find the answer on her computer.

I feel cheered at the idea of having something to talk to her about, of having an excuse to draw her out from the crowd, of maybe taking a little walk with her. The two of us. Like it used to be.

I change into my school clothes and grab my bag.

Dad's in the kitchen; he looks at me, one eyebrow raised.

'Thought I heard something last night,' he says.

'Yeah?'

He shrugs. 'Guess I must have been mistaken.'

'Guess so.'

I leave the house. The sun's out; it's already warm outside. For the first time in a long time I'm looking forward to going to school.

Conifers. You'd never think a few trees could cause so much trouble. When Yan's dad mentioned them, I didn't think anything of it. Trees. I mean, come on. Trees.

But as it turned out, the conifers were just the start of it. They were just the catalyst. Claire taught me that word. I like it. The catalyst is what ignites a situation. And the situation was definitely ignited. The fire raged for a long, long time.

None of it matters, not really, not in itself. But the conifers, like everything else, were one of the jigsaw pieces that made up the whole story. They got planted, then they grew. And then they grew some more and soon half our garden was in the shade. Mum's plants were dying one by one. She said it didn't matter, said that she'd plant new ones, said that the trees had a certain charm.

Dad disagreed.

It was around the same time that Yan's dad bought a new car. A Mercedes. Dad said it was a car for show-offs, for people who wanted to rub other people's noses in it.

I remember the first time he went round to Yan's house about the trees. Dad built himself up for days beforehand, paced around for ages arguing with Mum before he actually left the house. We waited in silence. I think Mum put the television on. We both knew what Dad would be like – he isn't much of a diplomat, really. He gets stressed-out in confrontations, and to hide it he goes in all guns blazing. I imagined Yan's mum offering him some lovely food or something and him just shouting at her. It made me cringe. I think it was the first time I ever cringed at my dad, ever wished he wasn't exactly who hewas, realised that he had flaws. Quite major ones, actually.

I sometimes wonder what would have happened if he hadn't shouted, if he'd talked in a reasonable way, found a compromise, explained the problem rationally like they teach you to do in PSHE classes at school. Would everything be different? Then again, there's no point thinking like that, is there? Things aren't ever different; they are what they are.

So anyway, when he came home we knew immediately it hadn't gone well; there was no triumphant smile, no raised arms waiting for us to hug and congratulate him. The door just opened; he came in, walked into the sitting room, sat down and picked up the paper, which was where he'd left it on the coffee table. Not a word was spoken. Mum looked over at him anxiously, but didn't say anything either. I don't know how long we all sat there like that – I think eventually Dad got up and huffed his way into the kitchen. Mum followed him and they had a conversation in stressed voices. I just carried on watching television. I figured it was nothing to do with me.

So that was the conifers. One nil to Yan's dad.

Only it didn't stop there.

It never does, does it?

Two weeks later, Yan's dad came round. Mum opened the door – I was watching telly again, sitting on the sofa, so I could see them talking out on the porch. Initially he sounded tense, angry, but Mum just kept talking in a low voice and soon she was smiling, he was smiling. I figured everything was OK again. That was Mum's role in arguments; Dad had the argument and Mum made things nice again. She did it with me, when Dad had been having a go, when he'd lost his temper and said things he hadn't meant. Hadn't meant according to Mum, that is. She always made out things were OK.

So there they were talking, when Dad's car pulled up in the drive. He got out and immediately his shoulders tensed; I could see his face, could see the way his jaw was set. I got up off the sofa and edged towards the door.

Mum smiled at Dad, her 'silent communication' smile, like the one she'd shoot at me if Grandma said something stupid and Mum didn't want me to point it out.

'We've had a little summit,' she said, her eyes twinkling. 'The conifers are going to be trimmed back and I said that I'd help them with a bit of gardening some time if –'

She didn't get to finish the sentence. Dad marched towards her and pushed her into the house. Then he grabbed Yan's dad by the arm and pulled him away.

'You stay away from my family, you bastard,' he shouted. 'You stay away.'

'But your wife, she asked me to –'

And that's when Dad punched him. I watched it, open-mouthed. Yan's dad was thrown to the floor and Dad didn't even look at him; he came into the house and slammed the door.

'Chloe? Where the hell are you?' he yelled, then marched to the kitchen when she replied. The door closed. I heard Mum shout, then gasp, then cry. Then Dad came out again, pushed past me into the sitting room and sat down.

'And you can bugger off too,' he said, sitting down heavily on the sofa and picking up the remote control, changing the channel, switching to a football game instead of *The Simpsons*.

'Don't tell your son to bugger off,' Mum said, appearing at the door. Her face was red and blotchy. I thought it was tears. It wasn't till the next day I saw the bruises.

'I'll say what I like to who I like.'

'You're speaking, are you? I thought you'd dispensed with speaking. I thought it was all action now.'

I'd never heard my mum sounding so sarcastic, so angry. Her eyes were almost black.

'I'm warning you, Chloe.'

'Warning me? Oh, I've been warned, don't worry. It's not the bloody trees, is it? This has got nothing to do with the trees. You're a bigot.'

'A bigot?' Dad's face started to go red. 'People are losing their jobs, their homes. Our economy is in the shit.' He looked at the wall that sat between our house and Yan's. 'And people like him, they come and they buy us up cheap, then lord it over us. They're laughing at us, Chloe. Laughing at you.'

'You sound exactly like Patrick.' Her eyes were stony now.

'That's because Patrick talks sense. People have had enough of being second-class citizens in their own country.'

'Is that what Patrick says?'

'It's what I say. And if you have that man round here again, you're going to regret it, do you understand?'

'Perfectly,' Mum said. Her eyes fell on me and I saw a desperate sadness in them. Thinking about it, that was the beginning of it. Her depression. Her disengagement. After that her eyes never really lost the sadness underneath.

I get to school early. I'll get breakfast at the canteen, I decide, then hang around in the classroom. We've got double English this morning – Claire will be there. I'll just be there when she walks in. Maybe she'll come and sit next to me.

I'm walking towards the gate with a spring in my step. I cross the road, vaguely keeping an eye out for traffic. My arms are swinging at my side, I feel light, unencumbered. I feel like a normal person. For the first time in a very long time.

And then I see someone on the other side, next to the school gates, and my stomach clenches slightly. It's one of them. I know it immediately.

I look away. I tell myself he doesn't exist. If I can just get inside the school gates I'll be safe. I'll find Claire, we'll laugh about things, things will be normal.

But I know I'm kidding myself. He's looking right at me, and I know I won't make it. Know in the pit of my stomach. I feel sick. I want to scream, 'I'm not a freak. My dreams are from History lessons, from the History Channel. You have nothing on me.'

The lightness, the happiness, the double English, the smiles are all receding. He's been waiting for me. I can't get into school without passing him, without being hooked. His face is grim, his eyes hollow like the rest of theirs'. Like he hasn't slept in a year, like he's come out of a Russian novel, one about people being sent to Siberia. He's walking towards me now; I can't stop because I'm in the middle of the road. I'm trapped. He's between me and the place I want to be. I consider running, like a rugby forward. Would he tackle me to the ground if I did? I'm sure he wouldn't. I don't even have to run. I'm just going to walk right past. Pretend he doesn't exist.

I see Claire inside the gates and my heart lurches; she's talking to a friend, her face bright. She's laughing. She looks up and sees me; she waves. I wave back, but I feel as if she's on the shore and I'm at sea. She thinks I'm waving to say hello, but really I'm drowning, like in that poem we read once in English. She grins then turns and walks through the door with her friend, into the school. She's gone. I'm on my own.

I put my head down, walk purposefully. I'm nearly there. Nearly at the gate. I'll be safe once I'm inside. The freaks haven't got into the school yet.

'Will? Will, I have to talk to you.'

He knows my name. No big deal. Keep walking. Just keep walking.

He's moving; he's in front of me, blocking my way. Not a rugby tackle, but still effective. I try to push him away but I know it's hopeless, know deep down that I can't run, can't hide. Why? Why can't I?

'Leave me alone,' I seethe.

'Will, we have to talk. It's important.'

I don't say anything and walk the other way, but he

sticks to me like an annoying younger sibling.

'Will, it's for your own good. You must be suffering. We can help. You must understand who you are.'

I swing round. 'I know who I am,' I bark. 'I'm Will Hodges. If you don't leave me alone, I'm going to call the police.'

The man smiles sadly. 'The police can't help you, Will. Only we can. Do you dream, Will? Do you dream of terrible things?'

I stop. My heart's racing.

Then I shake myself. It was just a lucky guess. Everyone has dreams. And anyway, I know what mine mean now.

'Dreams about the past? About death and destruction?' he persists. 'Do you wake, desperate and broken and unable to sleep? Do you, Will?'

I'm sweating. I'm looking at him. I hate him. I hate him more than I've ever hated anyone. How does he know about my dreams? Why is he trying to turn me back into a freak? I'm normal. I'm normal. People are walking past us into the school – classmates, other pupils. No one's even looking at us.

'You can't just do this to people.' I'm trying a different tactic now. I'm begging. 'Please,' I say. 'Please leave me alone. You don't know what it's like having you following me all the time. Do it to someone else, OK? Do it to her.'

I point randomly at a girl walking into the school, chatting on her mobile phone; she looks as though she doesn't have a care in the world.

'She's not a Returner, Will. You are,' the man says. He takes my arm. At his touch, I'm drowning again. I'm going under. I know. I know.

I won't go back. I want to stay here. I won't do it. You can't make me.

I struggle free, pull my arm away. 'I'm not a Returner. I'm Will Hodges.' I sound less convincing than before.

'Now you are. But that's not the end of the story, Will, and you know it.'

Yes, I do. I know. I know deep down. I've always known.

I shake myself. He's doing this to me. That's how they suck people in. I've watched programmes on cults. They brainwash you.

'Come with me, Will. Please. Just hear me out. I can see you're confused and drained. You must be feeling so alone. We're here for you, Will. We are the same as you. We know. Let us help you. Let us help you remember.'

'I don't want to remember.' I hear my voice as though it is someone else's.

Her eyes. Make her stop. Send her away. I can't . . . The ice is cracking. My body; it's cracking into two. The pain . . . the searing pain . . .

'You have to remember. It is the only way.'

'No.' I bend over in pain. Pain from what? I want to curl into a little ball. Now people *are* looking, but I don't care any more.

'Yes.' He holds out his hand. A lifeline. A noose. I

am shaking. I am not the person I was ten minutes ago. I don't know where that Will, that happy confident excited Will, has gone.

I look at the man. I take his hand and allow him to help me up.

He has won.

CHAPTER TWELVE

We walk into town in silence. I follow him into a coffee shop. It's a normal coffee shop, one of those ones that sells fifteen types of coffee, where you have to speak Italian just to order something. It's not busy – a couple of harassed-looking people in suits queuing up, a man with a laptop at a table, two women with babies. It feels so normal. I wonder what would happen if I shouted, if I pointed at the man and told everyone he'd brought me here against my will.

He didn't bring me here against my will, though. I followed him.

I still don't know why.

Do I?

I'm too hot. I shrug off my jacket. Still hot. Prickly under my shirt. The man is talking to me. I'm not listening. He tries again; I do my best to concentrate.

'Drink, Will? Do you want something to drink?'

I shake my head. Then I nod. 'Water,' I say. 'A bottle of water.'

He orders and we make our way to a table. I open the water, guzzle it down like I haven't drunk anything for days, like I've been trekking across the desert or something.

'Now what?' I ask sullenly when the man doesn't say anything. I feel stupid, as though I've walked into a trap; I should have known better.

'Just wait, Will. The others are coming.'

'The others?' I wipe my forehead, drink some more water. I'm burning up. What have I done? There's still time to leave, to walk away. But I'm not going anywhere. I know that.

We wait.

I drum my fingers on the table.

The girl is the first to arrive – the girl from the shopping centre and the river. She smiles at me, a hopeful smile, the sort of smile you give someone after an argument when you've tentatively made up, when you want them to be your friend again. I don't smile back. She's not my friend.

And yet . . . perhaps she was once; some residual memory, an image . . .

No. I give myself a mental kick. No, I don't remember her, I don't know her at all. It's my mind playing tricks. Any feeling of familiarity is a mirage, is false memory.

She sits down on the other side of me. I'm cornered. I look at the door. I look at the other people.

The man with the laptop takes out his phone. All so normal.

Two more people arrive – a man and a woman. The young woman from my garden. I shrink back; she smiles, her eyes still ghostly sad. I clutch my water bottle – it's empty, but it's something to hold on to.

'More water, Will?' the man asks.

I don't want anything from them. I put my hand in my pocket – as usual I find money in there. It suddenly disturbs me that I don't know where the money is coming from. Then an idea comes to me. Dad – maybe he puts the money in my pocket. Maybe it's his way of looking after me. This thought makes me feel good, makes me feel stronger. He cares. Dad cares about me.

I hand the man a couple of pound coins. 'Thanks.'

He looks slightly hurt at the gesture, but takes the money and goes back to the counter. Three more people arrive – two men, one woman. The men are old, much older. The woman is maybe thirty, I'd guess. They cram round the table; it occurs to me that we should have sat somewhere with more room.

The man comes back, gives me my water. I open it hurriedly and drink half of it in one go. Then I look up.

'So?' I say. My voice is shaking. My whole body is shaking.

'So,' the man from outside the school gates says. 'I suppose you want to know what this is all about.'

I shrug. 'I want to know why you all follow me,' I

say, reddening as I speak. 'I want to know . . .'

'How we know you, Will?' His voice is kind. Warm. I hadn't noticed that before.

'Yeah,' I agree. 'How you *think* you know me.' I put my bottle of water on the table and look round at them defiantly.

The man looks at the others; their glances give him the go-ahead to speak for them.

'This is difficult,' he says, 'because the situation is unprecedented. You are a Returner, Will. You are . . .' He sighs. 'Everyone here is a Returner. We . . . We return. Again and again. But never before has someone . . . We've been looking for you, Will. You've been absent for a very long time. When news of your return came, we – some of us – came to see you, to welcome you back. But you didn't remember, Will.'

'You didn't think maybe you'd got it wrong?' I ask. I'm getting that drowning feeling again. Sinking. Falling. I resist it. I'm not going under. I look at the man stonily. 'What do you mean by "return" anyway? Where from? How?'

The man's face crumples slightly. He looks at the girl from the mall and she leans forward.

'We return, Will. We live, we die, we return.'

I won't go back. Back where?

I raise an eyebrow. 'You mean you believe in reincarnation?' I say dismissively. 'Right, well, not my bag.' I pull myself up but I feel a hand on my arm; it's hers. I feel an electrical current shoot through me; I sit down again and she lets go.

'Not reincarnation. Not like other people think of it,' she says. Her voice is soft but insistent. 'We *actually* come back, Will. We've existed throughout time. We experience the worst that humankind is capable of; we absorb the pain, contain the horrors. We remember, Will. We are humanity's conscience.'

'Horrors? What horrors?' Still the sullen tone; they're not getting me without a fight.

'Horrors, Will. You know what I'm talking about.' She looks at me, into my eyes. I can see it. I know. I look away.

'No, I don't know,' I say.

'What about your dreams, Will?' Her hand returns to my wrist. I flinch.

'Everyone dreams.'

'Returners' dreams are different.' She smiles sadly. 'We dream humankind's history,' she says, her voice almost a whisper. 'All the pain, all the suffering, all the brutality. You have those dreams too, don't you, Will?'

I'm going under. I can feel the water in my lungs.

'I dream about History lessons. Dad watches the History Channel.' I cringe at myself as I speak. I have to keep fighting.

'It's not easy remembering,' the girl continues. Her voice is soporific; it could send me to sleep. No, that's what they want. They want me to sleep, to slip under the water without knowing it, to let them pull me under.

'I don't remember. OK?' My dreams. Chunks of time I can't account for. Details I remember but shouldn't. I force these thoughts from my head and notice that my left hand is screwed into a tight fist.

'It's a burden that we carry,' she soothes me. 'We need each other, Will. We help each other. You must let us help you.'

'I don't need your help. I don't remember anything. I don't know what you're talking about.'

I'm seeing death, I am amongst it, I hear tormented cries. Are they mine?

No! No, they were dreams. Only dreams.

'You've been alone for a long time, Will. You've been off the earth with no one around you. You were missing for nearly fifty years.'

'Missing? What are you talking about?'

I know what they're talking about. I don't want to remember. I am afraid of remembering. I won't go back. Let me stay. I won't be a part of it any more. I can't be.

'We die, Will, and we come back. Often straight away. Sometimes we come back after a short period. Perhaps our souls need to rest, to recuperate. Six months, a year. You were gone for a very long time, Will.'

I turn to look at her. I need to focus. Need to ground myself in reality. 'You're saying that you think I'm a Returner, that I live and come back, right?'

She nods.

'And the last time I – the person you think I am – was alive was fifty years ago?'

'Longer than that. It took nearly fifty years for you

to come back, Will. You've been back a while now.'

I shake my head. 'No,' I say firmly. 'No. This is stupid. Ridiculous. Whatever you're trying to do to me, I'm not having it. OK? I don't want anything to do with you. I don't want –'

'Do you remember, Will? Do you remember where you were?'

I bury my face in my hands.

'Do you dream about it, Will? Do you smell the ash? Do you see the horror?'

The smoke. Spiralling up into the sky. The queues of desperate people. The stench of death.

'No.' I clamp my hands over my ears.

'The bodies piled up. You remember them, Will. You remember.'

Bones on one pile, possessions on another – gold teeth, jewellery, a walking stick.

I won't go back. Can't go back. I am not ready. Still not ready.

'I don't remember!' I push the table back, my voice a roar. 'I don't remember.'

I stand up, looking at the faces around the table, seeing the pain in their eyes. The girl behind the counter glances at me then looks away. I am crying. I sink back into my chair. My head falls on to the table; my arms cover it. 'I don't remember,' I sob. 'I don't remember.'

A hand on my shoulder, another on my head – friendship, understanding, I feel it all, like osmosis through my skin.

'You will,' the girl says. 'And when you do, we'll be here, Will. We'll always be here.'

I sit like that for a long time. I don't know how long – it feels like hours but it could be just minutes.

'I have the same eyes as you.'

These are the first words I say when I finally sit up again. It's the first time I have admitted it. I have seen them in the mirror, a warning I have chosen to ignore until now.

'Eyes that have seen things,' the man says.

'I still don't remember,' I say flatly. I am defeated. 'I have the dreams. But I don't . . .'

'No,' he says, shaking his head. 'No, you don't remember. I can see that.'

'So why?' I ask. 'Why don't I?' I am still wary, still want to run. But I know I can't. I know I won't.

He looks bewildered. 'As I've said, Will, it is unprecedented. But perhaps . . . perhaps it was too much for you. Perhaps you are trying to escape from your fate.'

'You think I'm running away? You think I'm pretending?' My anger flares up.

'No.' Again, a hand on mine. Soothing. Calming. 'No, Will. It's not you. It is your subconscious, your inner Returner. It's not running away. Perhaps you still need time, that is all.'

I digest this for a few minutes.

'So you're all like normal people? When you're

137

not doing this Returner stuff.'

'Doing this Returner stuff?' The man looks perplexed.

The girl from the shopping centre smiles. 'It's not *Doctor Who*,' she says. There's a twinkle in her eye. It looks strange. Strange but in a good way. 'We don't "do Returner stuff". We just live. And . . .'

She looks around the table.

'And what?' I demand.

'And absorb,' one of the other women offers. She's older. Fifty or so. Speaks with a foreign accent.

'Absorb the horrors. Yeah, you said that.'

The girl swallows awkwardly; the woman looks away. I stare at the man. The man who brought me here. 'I still don't know what you're on about.'

He looks at me gravely. 'Where there is distress, where there is cruelty and desperation, there are Returners, to absorb it, to remember it, to protect humanity from itself.'

I don't say anything for a few minutes. 'You mean I'm here to suffer? You mean I'm *going* to suffer? That's what I'm here for? That's why I exist?'

I notice bruises on the girl's hand all of a sudden. Why didn't I see them before? I pull up her sleeve – more bruises. Burns.

The woman with the accent. She hasn't got a hand. She's missing one.

My eyes move from one to the other, jumping, afraid to see, *needing* to see. The man leans forward.

'Suffering is relative,' he says. 'Some of us suffer the

pain of a thousand small cuts, others . . .' He smiles sadly. 'We cannot know when or how . . .'

I see my dream again. The last one. The one Claire couldn't place. *Screaming, shouting. A loud bang. Something falling against me; a woman. A woman with long hair, she looks like my mother. No, not like her. Just the hair. She is looking at me, she is bleeding, clutching at me, her face full of shock, of fear. 'This must end.' She is sinking down to the floor. I can't help her. I am hot. I am sweating. I am screaming. No. No! NO!*

Is this my fate? Is this where I'm headed?

I bang my fists on the table. I stand up again, boxing the dream, the emotion, the fear. 'Well, thanks for this.' Cocky. Sarcastic. It feels good, like I'm wresting control. I'm myself again. Me, Will. Outsider, freak maybe, but not one of them. I'm my own person. 'Really enlightening. So glad to have met you all. But to be honest, I'm not interested. I don't want to be a Returner. Doesn't really fit with my life plan, if you know what I mean. So thanks for the water and for the . . .' I glance at the girl and flinch slightly. 'The information,' I say. 'But I think I'll be going now.'

'You can go, Will, but you can't change what you are. You can't change your destiny.'

'A destiny which involves hideous pain? Yeah, well, I'll take my chances,' I say. I push the table a little too fiercely; the man is forced back on his chair. He stands up; the others shift so that I can get out. I walk to the door, not looking back. Then I open it, feel the fresh air on my face. And then I run. I run as fast as I can. I don't know where I'm going. I don't know what I'm running from. I just know I cannot stop until my chest constricts, until I am gasping for air, until my body can't run any more.

CHAPTER THIRTEEN

I walk around for a while. I think at some point I eat something. I'm not really aware of time passing, but I must be at some level because at four fifteen I'm at the school gates waiting for Claire. She'll have just finished History of Art. Soon I'll see her coming out of the swing doors to the side of the main building, walking towards me, her hair streaming out behind her, tamed but only slightly. She has red curls; she plaits them sometimes but usually lets them do their own thing under a hairband that keeps them off her face. She straightened it once – it looked awful and I told her. I like her hair the way it is. I like that it doesn't obey the rules.

She sees me and I see something cross her face. Pleasure? Surprise? I'm not sure. I want to know. I walk towards her.

Not pleasure or surprise. Concern. Her brow is

creased. It makes my stomach lurch. It's creasing for me. Just for me.

'Will? Are you OK? Where have you been all day?' She walks towards me quickly.

'You know you're meant to go to school and go to lessons,' she says archly.

I shrug. She takes my arm. 'Will, what's going on?' She's peering at me; I look away. I'm conscious of my eyes, don't want her seeing that I look like *them*, like the freaks. I can't call them by their name.

We walk along the road and pause at the junction. Left is home, right is into town. We turn right. Then we head left out towards the river. Neither of us says anything. We walk until we come to the bench I always sit on. She sits down first; I wait a moment, then follow. I take a deep breath.

'So?' she says.

'So,' I say. I exhale loudly, put my elbows on my knees. Then I look at her tentatively. 'Do you think I'm a freak?'

She frowns. 'I think you're a bit freaky sometimes.'

There's the hint of a smile on her lips. It immediately reassures me, calms me. She is normal. If I hold on to her I will float, I will stay on the surface.

'And . . .' I hesitate. Once I start this, I won't be able to go back, won't be able to erase it. I tell her and that's it. 'Do you believe in reincarnation?'

Her frown deepens. 'Reincarnation? You mean people coming back as flies if they live a bad life and as a princess if they're good?'

'Just coming back,' I say. 'Do you believe humans – some humans – can come back? That they return?'

'That they return?' She's trying to take me seriously, trying to come up with a considered answer. 'Have you found religion, Will?'

I shake my head. I'm getting agitated. 'Forget it.' I stand up; her hand pulls me back down.

'Explain,' she insists. 'Tell me what you mean. Give me context.'

Context? I sit back against the back of the bench, close my eyes, let the late afternoon sun warm my face. Sitting here I can almost forget. I open my eyes again. And then I see him, on the other side of the river. He was there this morning, at the coffee shop. One of the older men. He's looking at me, the usual mournful expression on his face. He turns and walks slowly away.

I am short of breath. I grab Claire.

'He's one of them,' I say, pointing.

'One of who?' she asks.

'The Returners,' I say. 'The Returners.'

It takes me a long time to explain it. I make a few false starts – Claire's looking at me like I need to be put away, locked up somewhere. But then she starts to listen properly. I tell her about the people following me around, about the eyes, about this morning. I tell her what they told me, tell her they knew about my dreams. I don't tell her I am one. I'm not. But I do tell her that they think I'm one of them. I say it in a way that leaves a way out, that waits for her to tell me it's preposterous, that I couldn't be one, that they're freaks, just like I've always thought.

Instead, she looks out over the river.

'Mum has always said you're an old soul,' she says quietly, thoughtfully. 'She always says you've lived more than a boy your age should have.'

I stare at her. 'You believe them? You think I'm a freak?'

'Do you?'

I look away irritably.

'You used to tell me about the people watching you. I remember seeing them, Will.'

'You saw them?' My throat feels constricted all of a sudden, strangled. 'You never told me.'

'I thought you'd get even more upset. But I did, I know I did. What you said about their eyes, it made me remember.'

Claire looks strange. I *feel* strange. I swallow with difficulty. I open my mouth to speak, close it again then gear up and force myself to speak. This is worse than talking to the shrink. With him I was all front. Now I have no front. Now I have nowhere to hide.

'They said,' I say carefully, 'that they're here to suffer. They basically lead hideous lives, full of pain and agony. Then they die and come straight back for more crap.'

My voice is shaking slightly. Cracking.

Claire puts her hand over mine. She presses down,

calms me. 'And you don't remember anything?'

I shake my head. 'Just the dreams.' I have never felt so vulnerable. I feel like I've taken off my skin.

'The dreams.' Claire nods as though it all makes sense.

'You actually believe all this crap?' I ask, a last stand against defeat.

'Do you think it's why you're so angry?' she asks. 'Because you've suffered so much?'

I pull my hand away. 'I'm not angry.'

Claire says nothing; her silence is enough.

'I'm not,' I say again.

'The other dream, the one we couldn't place. Do you think it's . . . ?'

She doesn't finish the sentence. She doesn't need to.

'My destiny?' I ask.

She's silent for a moment or two. 'The future,' Claire says quietly.

'I don't know.' I stand up. 'I don't care. I don't want anything to do with it. I don't want to be a Returner. It sucks. It's the shittiest job in the whole world. So I'm not going to. I refuse. OK? I refuse.'

'You think it works like that?' Claire asks, standing up too.

'I don't care how it works.'

'Why did you forget, do you think? They said you were missing for fifty years?'

We're walking now, back towards town.

'Yeah. I wish I'd stayed away for longer.'

'Did they say where you were? Before?'

*I smell the dust, see the piles of bones, the trinkets.
Her eyes are no more and yet they still bore into me. I
am winded. I stop, bend over, catch my breath; my
head is pounding. I crouch down on the ground. I
want to cry out, to roar. No more. No more. Never
again. I run. I throw myself against the fence. A jolt, a
current. Then release. I won't go back. I won't Return.*

'Will? Will?' Claire is on the ground next to me,
taking my hand, feeling my head. 'Will, what's
happening? What's the matter?'

I breathe: in and out. Push the images from my
mind. I let Claire help me up.

I look at her. I can feel my expression. It's like
theirs. Sad. Reproachful. Tired. Heavy. I don't want
to remember. But I know they are coming, know the
memories are waves that cannot be stopped. I have
built a dam and now it is breaking, bit by bit. They
will wash over me, they will carry me away, and I
cannot escape from them.

'They think it might have been Auschwitz,' I say, as
lightly as I can. The word is a flash in my head, a
flash of white light, of pain, excruciating pain. 'They
think that whatever happened, they think I took a
long time to get over it, to come back,' I say. The
waves are coming. All I can do is prepare myself. All I
can do is try my best to surface.

People think Dad started drinking after Mum died. By
'people' I mean Grandma and Grandad. They used to

come round a lot after, but then they stopped. I think Dad fell out with them too. Even though they're his parents, not hers. Mum didn't have any parents. Not since I was born anyway. Her dad died of a heart attack when she was pregnant and her mother went soon after. Went. That was Dad's word, the word he used when he explained why I only had one set of grandparents. It was an odd word to use, I remember thinking. When you die, you don't go anywhere; you do the opposite. You stop. There are no more journeys.

Little did I know. Guess back then I hadn't figured on being a Returner.

Anyway, it wasn't true, about Dad and his drinking. The drinking started earlier. When he lost his job, when he stopped being the man in the smart suit and the smart car. It happened a few years after we moved here. A year or so before Yan moved next door. Back then, no one really noticed the large glass of whisky sloshed down before dinner, the bottle of wine drunk during. But then, then the conifers came and our bin clinked all the time with empty bottles, bottles he'd stuff at the bottom but which were still there, even if you couldn't see them.

He was better for a while after he got a new job. Mostly, anyway. He only really drank when he went out with Patrick. And then he only did it to be sociable, he said.

But after the big fight with Yan's dad, you could smell it on his breath again a lot of the time. He'd be more erratic – happier sometimes, which was great; he'd pick me up and swing me around his shoulders, which he never used to do because he had a bad back, but sometimes not happy at all. He started to get into moods – not the white anger I knew and could deal with, but worse, like dark clouds were sitting on his head and he couldn't see past them. He wouldn't notice if I walked into the room, or maybe he chose not to notice. He'd notice soon enough if I changed the channel on the telly, would stand up and swipe the remote out of my hand, giving me a clip round the ear at the same time. Mum would leave him alone; she'd talk in hushed tones, and would pretend that everything was OK, that he was just stressed because of work, but I knew that wasn't true. I saw the empty glass bottles on the floor next to him, knew that drinking straight out of the bottle was wrong, that it meant something even though I couldn't put my finger on exactly what.

The first time I saw a bruise on Mum's face, she said she'd been clumsy like always and she rolled her eyes at herself. I believed her too. And the time after that. And then one day I came back from Claire's early and Mum and Dad were having a big fight and I saw him. I saw him hit her and she fell down, but then she saw me, through the window, and she got up quick as she could and smiled and made out like nothing had happened.

Later that evening, when I was having a bath, she

told me that Dad just got upset sometimes, that he misunderstood things and got the wrong end of the stick. But he didn't mean to get angry. It just wasn't easy being a dad when the world was such a difficult place. He was doing his best for us.

And I remember nodding and thinking about it, and thinking that maybe it was hard but if he ever hit my mother again I would kill him.

CHAPTER FOURTEEN

I get back home, eventually, my mind in a blur. I have to get upstairs. Have to get to my bedroom, to safety. I am scared. No, not scared. It's something deeper. Everything is going to change. I am like a caterpillar – I need a cocoon, need to find somewhere safe to go for my metamorphosis. Into what? Back to who I am. What I am.

'Will? That you?' Dad is at home. I open the door to the sitting room – he is on his chair. He has been drinking; I smell it immediately. I glance at my watch – 8.45 p.m. He sees my eyebrows shoot up. 'And where the hell have you been?' he asks angrily.

I avoid his eyes. I need to curtail the conversation. 'Just out with a couple of mates,' I say evasively.

'You? Mates?' He is joking, laughing at me, and I am immediately flooded with resentment. It's his fault. It's all his fault. But I bite my tongue. 'Which mates?'

'Greg. Tim,' I lie. There's a Greg in the year above me; I've never spoken to him. But he will do.

'Greg?' Dad doesn't believe me. I should have picked another name. 'School friends, are they?'

I nod.

'So you've been at school then?'

'Yeah. Look, Dad, I need to –'

'So why the bloody hell did I get a call from the head's office?' Dad interrupts. 'Telling me this is the second time this week you haven't been in at all?'

His eyes are flashing with anger, not black humour.

'You're a bloody waster.' He is on a roll now. 'You've got exams next year. Think your mother would be proud of you bunking off school like this?'

I close my eyes. Don't listen. Cut this short and get away.

'She thought so much of you. But she never saw the real you, did she? Will the loser. Who can't even go to school, let alone pass an exam. What do you think she'd have made of you, Will? What do you think she'd say now?'

He's been drinking. I try to breathe, try to contain the anger welling up inside me. I can rise above his words. One of us has to rise above it. Otherwise we both know how this is going to end. It's not even the hitting I'm worried about – it's the sobbing afterwards, the apologies, the telling me it'll never happen again when I know it will. Because it always does.

'This has got nothing to do with Mum,' I say, controlling my voice as best I can. 'I've had some . . .

some stuff going on. I didn't go to school today. I'm sorry, Dad. But I'll go tomorrow. I'll be OK.'

'You'll be OK?' He rolls his eyes. 'You think I'm worried about you being OK? All the years I've sacrificed, looking after you. And for this? This is how you pay me back?'

I edge backwards. I have to get out. The walls of the sitting room are pressing in on me.

'Where d'you think you're going? You're not going anywhere, my boy. You're going to tell me what you've been doing. Who you've been hanging around with. Have you been breaking the law? Drinking? Taking drugs? Have you?'

I shake my head. 'It's nothing like that, Dad.'

He moves closer to me. 'Maybe she knew. Maybe she suspected you'd turn out like this. Maybe that's what pushed her over the edge, Will. Ever thought about that?'

I stare at him angrily. I can feel the white heat descending. 'Don't,' I say. It is a warning. I have never warned my father before.

'Don't?' He raises his eyebrows. 'You're a let-down, Will. You're a waste of space. You've had everything. Every opportunity, and look at you.'

'I'm going upstairs, Dad. You're drunk.' I feel older than him. I find myself thinking that he is the let-down, not me.

'Drunk? Do you blame me?' He stands up, stumbles towards me. 'With you as a son? Do you really blame me?'

I close my eyes. I breathe, count to ten. Then I leave the room. I walk to the kitchen, pour myself a glass of water. I drink it, then calmly make myself some toast. I smear peanut butter on it; it will do for supper. I wolf it down. I realise how hungry I am and make two more slices. I pour another glass of water; I am in control. Methodical. Nothing else matters. I head out of the kitchen towards the stairs.

Through the living room door I can see Dad lying on the ground. With a sigh, I walk in. He has fallen. I roll him over; he has a black eye coming – he must have hit something on the way down. I look at him for a few moments, puzzled. Then I go back to the kitchen for some frozen peas. I crouch over him and press the peas to his head, like I saw Mum do once when things with Yan's dad had really deteriorated. Lawyers and black eyes do not go well together, she'd said.

He opens his eyes; he is looking at me warily. I recognise the look in his eye, or remember it – I have seen it before, but I can't remember where. He pushes me away, but he has little strength.

Yan's brother. He has the same expression as Yan's brother. Confused. Uncertain. Fearful. It unsettles me; I am not used to my father looking any of these things.

'You need to hold this,' I say, putting his hand where mine has been on the peas.

He grunts something, pushes my hand away. I let go, watch him for a second to make sure he's holding them right, then stand up and make my way up to my room.

Once there, I close the door, put a chair up against it, then turn off the light and get into bed, only taking off my clothes once I'm under the duvet.

It is time to know the truth. It is time to face the suffering, to look into the eyes of whatever it was that kept me away for so long, that made me forget everything.

I am scared.

But I am ready.

Slowly, warily, I close my eyes. And gradually, bit by bit, sleep embraces me.

I am not Will any more.

I am a Returner.

The air is crisp, fresh and new. It is early morning – I can feel the dew in the air, under my feet. I'm running, running. My chest is hurting, I gasp for air. I stumble, but manage to land on my feet; I cannot afford to slow down. I must be quicker, must catch up. They are here. They are here somewhere. I have the coordinates, near enough, secured for me by one of my men. They are my men. I find the thought reassuring; it spurs me on. I am not used to running; I am used to waiting for information. But this is too important. I need to be there. I need to be seen there.

My radio is in my pocket – I want to reach down, to check it is working, for reassurance, but there is no time. If they are there, we must know now, before it is too late. We must be ahead of the game. I run. Across a field, through woodland.

They are clever, our enemy; they have thought this through. But they are not clever enough.

And they will pay for this. They are trying to destroy everything; they believe they can. But they will not. Eventually they will see; they will learn. We will teach them. We will show them the way. If they want to see it.

I see a break in the trees. I slow slightly; I am jogging now. I arrive at the clearing quietly, secretively. I must see the truth for myself. There is a camp – tents of varying sizes, a low murmur of human existence. There are large containers of water, some makeshift cubicles. Toilets? Showers? A larger tent – perhaps a food tent. Around these areas hundreds of people sit, walk, talk in hushed voices. There is worry in their eyes, exhaustion, concern. Children sit listlessly at their parents' sides. Those in charge are easy to identify – they walk, purposefully, armed with clipboards. They stop to check people, to peer into the mouths of the children, to point directions, to listen. They too appear exhausted, but they have a determination about them.

They are white. British. I know they are; I have done my research.

I also know that the others are not.

I try to work out the overall numbers – I cannot see into the tents, cannot see beyond this side of the camp. But from the resources, from the size of the water tanks, I can estimate. Between five hundred and a thousand. Perhaps even two thousand. There is enough to keep them here for a week perhaps. After that, what? Will more resources arrive? Is a departure date set?

I take out my radio, edge backwards so that I am not overheard. I relay the information. I give the coordinates. I feel reassured by the voice at the other end. They will be here. They will be here in minutes, not hours. I find a place to sit, hidden by some trees, a sprinkling of grass to soften the ground. I lower myself gently. And I wait until my men arrive.

My comrades. I know that I have their rapt attention – we are united in our cause. My cause. I have convinced them, over time, through skill and argument, and through offering a way out of their desperation. They are all desperate. Economic and social despair are fertile grounds for change. We sit, our voices hushed, discussing our strategy. I listen, I watch. Then I stand up and give the orders. I have decided. It is time.

We scatter; I am one of them. Their leader, but also their comrade. I am one of the people. Our people. We must fight the injustice, fight the unfairness. This is our land, the land of the free, of the righteous. We will reclaim it. We will make it our own again. I watch my men disappear and I feel proud, I feel excited. I have done this. I have made this happen.

We will stop the dissenters in their tracks. They think they are cleverer than us; they think that they can control things. But they can control nothing. We are ahead of them; we cannot be beaten. They will see. Eventually they will see.

A gunshot, another gunshot, the sound of people screaming, scattering. I will wait a few more minutes. More gunshots, shouting, running, more screaming. 'Help us, please help us.' 'You can't do this.' I listen and I wait. Slowly, order descends. Lines will have been formed, children brought into order, those hiding found. I wait . . . and then I stand up. I walk slowly towards the camp. I see the fear in the refugees' faces; I see the anger and outrage in the faces of those in charge of the camp. Our enemies. Terrorists. They are dangerous; they must be dealt with swiftly, to send a message. I watch as they are tied up. They thought they could hide here, thought we would not find them. They are foolish; I have no respect for them. Traitors. They cannot see the truth; will not see it.

Slowly, I walk towards them.

Somewhere else. Somewhere hot. Stifling. I am watching but I am not there. A man, not me, sits in a van. He is outside a school. Inside, the people wait. They are fearful, hungry, exhausted, but they have made it there; it reassures them. Elders walk around, reassuring, talking in low voices. The UN are here. They will protect us, they say.

Tall people. Like poppies. Their eyes have seen death, destruction; their legs have walked huge distances, children tied to their hips, to their backs. Their homes destroyed, their neighbours killed, everything gone.

We are safe here, they say.

They wait. Their shoulders unfreeze, just slightly. They begin to breathe a little more easily. They consider their futures, ask the questions they have had no time to ask themselves or their loved ones. Where will they go? What will happen when it is over? Will the deaths be avenged? How will they cope? How will they ever look each other in the eye again?

More arrive; the doors close behind them. Wounds are tended to. Screams from those who cannot be saved, weeping from those who love them.

A kind of order settles. Family groupings, village groupings.

The man gets out of the van. He signals to his friend. They walk towards the school.

Inside, the lights go out.

Another scene. Another place. A line of people. Pitiful, pathetic. They are broken already; they are the walking dead. Do they know that there is no future? Do they understand? The ash circles above. Mothers feed crusts to their children, hold one another for support. Their eyes are hollow, too large for their shrunken faces. I can smell disease, fetid flesh. The ash chokes my lungs. I bring my handkerchief to my mouth, covering my nose.

I look down the line; I look at their faces, their listless bodies.

The line is moving slowly.

I wipe a few beads of sweat away from my forehead.

I wake up and open my eyes. I am afraid. I don't want to go on. I sit up, swing my legs out of bed. I am panting. I am sweating. I go to the bathroom, splash water on my face. I catch my reflection in the mirror and shrink back. I don't want to go back to bed. I don't want to sleep. I walk around the house, but I know it's no use. I have to sleep. I have to know. I have to see, have to remember. If I don't, I will go mad, I will implode.

Heavily, I go back to my room. I shut the door. I get into bed.

I can't run any more. I have to face the pain, the agony. I must brace myself. Clenching my fists, I slowly close my eyes.

I am back at the camp, the moist English air like nectar as I breathe it in. They have seen me now, they are staring at me. All of them. I do not mind. I am used to the attention; I encourage it. Leadership. Direction. It is what we all need. It is my gift to my country. I give it willingly, a sacrifice of time and energy.

I do not rush; I let them wait as my footsteps bring me nearer, one by one.

'Who is in charge of this place?' I ask, when I am standing in front of them. A woman is pushed forward by one of my men. She has defiant eyes. Eyes that say she is right. But they are wrong; they do not realise the damage she is doing. It is too late for her to learn, but others will. Others will not follow in her path.

I look at her for a few seconds.

'How many people are there here?' I bark.

She says nothing. One of my men pushes a gun into her back.

'How many?' I ask again.

She braces herself. 'A thousand,' she says. She sounds proud. I shake my head pitifully.

'You bring a thousand people here? For what? Why?'

'To escape,' she says bitterly. 'To leave this god-forsaken place.'

'Godforsaken? No,' I say calmly, 'God has not forsaken us. You have. You and your treacherous followers.'

'Let them go. Let them go home.'

'Home? They say this is their home.'

'Let them leave. Let them leave if you despise them so much.'

'Why should I? They had their chance to leave and didn't take it.' My eyes are on hers, resting steadily. She looks down.

'They have done nothing wrong.'

I shake my head again. 'No, that is not true. And if they leave, they will come back. Others will come. I have evidence on my side. What do you have?'

'Humanity,' she says.

I allow myself a laugh.

'Humanity,' I say. 'No. You don't see the truth. You won't. We have to protect our land, protect our people. You set up a camp for these intruders when our own people are starving.'

'They aren't starving.' She is angry now. 'They may be jobless, but they're not starving. We don't know what it is to be starving.'

'Enough!' I glare at her; two of my men take her arms, hold them behind her.

The hot place again. I am there but not there. An onlooker? No, further away than that. And yet I see everything. The people look around in fear. Switches are flicked. The electricity has failed. A wail erupts but is immediately stopped. Reassuring voices are heard. It will come back. It is not a problem. Don't panic. We are safe here, they say, we are protected. We were told to come, and we came, and now we are safe. Do not worry. Do not be alarmed by the lights going off. We will find candles. This is not a problem.

Hearts that were racing begin to slow slightly. There is nodding, agreement. It is important not to panic. The panic is over. The horror is behind them.

Men stand protectively in front of their wives, their children.

Water, a child says. I need some water.

Water. Yes. The father is relieved. Something to do. Something simple, something meaningful. I will go. I will find you some water.

He walks, out of the room, down a corridor. There is a line of people. I am looking for water, he says.

We are too, comes the reply.

Nodding, the father joins the line. He is holding an empty bottle. He is pleased with himself for bringing it, for having the presence of mind even as the mouth of hell opened up, as the men with their machetes and their hate and their rage descended. He holds it to him. And as he presses it to himself, he feels his chest constrict. He makes a sound, a sound he does not recognise. He feels tears on his cheeks The woman in front of him turns and looks at him. She nods, puts her hand on his shoulder. He has not cried since he was a little boy. He is ashamed. The woman shakes her head.

'We have seen what we should never have seen. What no one should see,' *she says.*

'My daughter . . .' *He cannot finish the sentence, cannot voice the terror, the pain he feels, that he will*

*always feel. His daughter. He no longer has a daugh-
ter. He has two sons; he saved them, they are here.
But his daughter . . . He was not quick enough to get
her out of their path. He holds the empty bottle of
water to him as though it were her, as though he has
been given a second chance.*

*But there are no second chances. He watched
them drive towards her, their machetes outstretched,
watched them cut her down, his own flesh and blood,
his little girl, tumbling to the floor lifeless.*

*And even now he finds himself grateful that this
was all they did, that they did not take her as they
had taken other girls, other women.*

*'I have no daughter. I have only sons now,' the
father says. He has to say it out loud. He cannot say
it to his wife.*

*The woman nods. 'I do not have a mother. I do not
have a father. I do not have a husband.'*

*His hand moves to hers and presses on it; they
stand like that for several minutes, more intimate
than he has ever been with anyone outside of his family. Then he lets go; she turns around. The moment is
over. Their grief cannot be lessened; but they have
been understood. That is something.*

*The father hears a commotion at the front of the
line; an argument has broken out. Even now, he
thinks, even in this dark time, people argue. Has
someone taken too much water? Spilled some?
Inadvertently insulted another in the line? The shouting gets louder; he walks forward.*

There are two men at the front of the line. One is banging the tap; the other is shouting at him. Then they switch positions, with the shouting man wrenching the tap and the other criticising him.

'What is the matter here?' the father asks. 'I'm sure we can resolve this in a friendly way.'

The men look at him; their eyes narrow. 'A friendly way?' one of them says. 'Tell me, friend, how do you resolve this? How do you resolve the fact that there is no water?'

'No water? You mean the tap is broken?'

The man shakes his head. 'It is not broken,' he says bitterly. 'I'm a plumber. There's nothing broken here. It's the mains. The water's been shut off.'

Another commotion, a man running down the corridor, his eyes wide with fear.

'What is it, brother?' the father asks. 'What has happened to you?'

'To me?' The man looks bewildered. 'Not to me. To us. To all of us. It's the doors. They are locked.'

'Yes, of course,' the father says patiently. 'We have locked the doors for our protection. To keep us safe.'

'No,' the man says. 'You do not understand. The doors are locked from the outside.'

Back to the lines of people. The ash is on my face, on my hands. The smell is overpowering. They feel it, they taste it. They are beginning to fret, to worry. They look at me anxiously. They hold out their hands, look at me with pleading eyes. I walk towards the door to confer with the guard. There has been a delay; there is more matter to dispose of than antici-pated. It will take an hour, maybe more. I glance back at the line; they are getting restless. A woman is crying, crying loudly; her fear will infect the others, she will cause problems. Her child starts to howl. The sound grates on my mind, like nails across a black-board. I bark at the guard. 'More men. Take some from the other line. Get it done quickly.'

I turn back to the woman, to the child. The woman stops; she sees the anger in my eye and hushes the child. But the child continues to wail. The mother looks at me in desperation. 'Please,' she mouths. 'Please, take him. Take my son.'

I look at her uncertainly.

'Please,' she says again, so quietly I can hardly hear. 'Please take him.'

I reach into my pocket.

I draw out my gun.

I wake up again, gripped with panic. But the images do not recede. They are no longer dreams. They are memories. The dam is open; they flood in and I can-not stop them. This is who I am. I cannot escape. I see them. I see it all.

It is Africa. I know. I don't know how I know, but I

know. A huddle of men are talking, separate from the other groupings. All around, families are holding each other in grief, trying to keep each other alive without water, without food.

'The UN will protect us. They will come,' the father says quietly. 'They told us to come here. They will come.'

Another shakes his head bitterly. 'We have been in this building for two weeks. The UN are not coming. If the UN were coming, they would be here by now. If the UN were coming, there would not be disease in this building and starving children. If they were coming, my son would be alive.'

'But,' the father says. 'But . . .' He is trying to think of rational reasons for the situation he finds himself in. He cannot – will not – accept a version of events where they are helpless, where there is no hope. He is a businessman. A logical man. The UN told them to come here. They would not do that unless there was a plan.

'But nothing,' the other man says. 'Why will you not see? They don't care about us. Nobody cares about us.'

'It isn't about whether they care,' the father says staunchly. 'It is about right and wrong. It is about . . .'

He is interrupted by a sound. Doors opening. He has never known such relief. 'You see?' he says. 'You see? They are here. They have come for us.'

But even as he speaks he can hear that things are not as they should be. A scream. Another scream. No reassuring voices telling everyone that the emergency is over. Instead, there is shouting. Angry shouting, the sound of . . . of . . . The father's chest constricts. He knows the sound. He heard it before, in his village.

'They are here. They are here with machetes. They are going to kill us all.'

The men look at each other. Then without a word they leave each other; they must return to their families. The father leaves the group and runs; he finds himself in the corridor with others, moving as fast as they can, falling against the wall, moaning as they slip to the floor. He finds his family where he left them; they are sleeping. So peaceful. He turns his wife over.

'My dear wife, you must wake up. There is something going on. There is . . .' He feels something wet against his leg. And when he sees what it is, he does not see. He will not. It is red paint. It is . . . It is . . .

'There. There is one.' He hears the shout too late, but he has nowhere to go to anyway. The man rushing towards him is a boy, younger than his own sons. He lunges at the father with his machete. 'You must die. Like vermin, you must die.'

The father nods and closes his eyes as he falls back against his wife, against his family.

The boy with the machete. He was in the van. Waiting. He has been waiting all this time.

* * *

I know this. I have been watching, waiting with him. Far from him, but with him all the same.

I am that boy. No, not that boy. I should have been him. I wouldn't go back. But I was meant to be there.

I am . . .

I get out of bed, somehow manage to pull on some clothes.

I can't close my eyes. Can't ever close my eyes again. Each blink is torture. Each blink takes me back, falling, into the abyss.

I was there. The place with the ash. The place with the piles of bones, piles of belongings. The places where humanity had ceased to exist long before. The places that suck the soul out of you.

I was there. In the other places, I was there . . .

But it's worse. So much worse.

My destiny is to suffer. To be a Returner. To feel man's pain, to absorb the desperation and the agony. That's what they said. That's what I was told.

No.

No, they didn't tell me the truth.

I do not suffer. I did not suffer.

I am on the ship. I look down and see the whip in my hand.

I am at the settlement, surrounded by dead bodies. Dead at my hand.

I am at the camp. I am in Poland. I am not in the line. I am not to be tortured, to be gassed to death for nothing but my very existence. I am the torturer. I am the murderer. I am the one sending them to their deaths.

I scream. My scream is silent. My tears are dry and yet my body shakes and shudders. I wrap my arms around myself. The horror. The horror. It was me. I am the horror. I am the devil. It was me.

I close my eyes. Immediately more images flood my mind.

I am the leader. I am at a march. Britain for Britons. Foreigners Out. British Jobs for British Workers. I am leading the rally. The time has come for change, the time has come to reclaim our lands. I am the designer of a new system of taxes, a new social strata. Different rules for immigrants, make it harder for them, make them want to leave. No access to services, no benefits, no healthcare or education. Turn the indigenous people against them. Blame them. It is their fault we are in this mess. They should go back to where they came from. We will make them. And if they don't go we will make them sorry. They will die here, in the land they have stolen from. They will be a lesson to the rest of the world. Great Britain will be great again. We will rise up triumphant.

I blink. I see it now. I am the leader of a holocaust. A future holocaust. I believe I am right. I convince others. I see the woman looking at me with hatred. I kill her. I burn the camp. I can hear the screams . . .

The woman tries to hand me her baby. I stare at her. Then I shoot.

I am at school. Yan's brother is looking up at me fearfully as I smash his face with my fist. Desperately he presses money into my hand – a five-pound note.

I am downstairs. Dad is on the ground; I have knocked him down.

I fall to my knees. I thought I was ready for the truth, but I was wrong. The truth is worse than anything I could have imagined.

I am the horror.

This is my destiny.

This is what I am.

CHAPTER FIFTEEN

Semi-dressed, I stumble downstairs, and go straight for Dad's drinks cabinet. Whisky. Whisky is what I want. I grab the bottle, tear off the lid and gulp. It is like fire in my throat, it tastes like petrol. I drink some more. I want the oblivion, want the denial that alcohol affords. I retch, but carry on.

I walk out of the house, carrying the whisky bottle at my side, bringing it to my mouth every few seconds.

'You didn't tell me the truth,' I shout. 'You told me I would suffer. You told me I was one of you.'

I continue to walk, continue to drink. My head is softening, my words blurring, dissolving into the night. I want to disappear. I want to go back to where I came from, back to nothingness. Fifty years wasn't long enough. I can see her eyes, staring up at me, the ash circling us. It was not the despair; it was not the desperation; not the pain or the final understanding of what was happening to her, to them all. It was the hope. In spite of everything, in spite of all my brutality, she was offering me her child. Hoping that I would take it, look after it, save it.

Me.

I remember it all now; remember how in that moment the ice cracked; the horror began to seep in, slowly, then more quickly, insistently. I couldn't keep it out, couldn't fill the holes it was flooding through. It was consuming me. I could remember too much, had seen too much. Too much for one soul.

An argument. I am shouting. Too much. I can't go back. I won't. I can't take it.

You must take it. That is what you are. You will find a way.

Why did I come back? So I could send some more people to the gas chambers? I don't know where I'm going; I'm walking unsteadily down the street, bumping into lamp posts. No, walking into them. I need the crash, need to feel the pain. Inhumane. I know what the word means now.

It means me. It defines me. I am evil. I am the bogeyman Mum was so afraid of.

I stop dead. Mum. I am clutching the bottle, gripping it tightly. It wasn't me. It wasn't me who . . .

Was it?

I fall to my knees. I cannot cry; I can only groan silently, my stomach full of bile. Did I kill her? Or did she kill herself because she knew, because she could see what I was?

I am in the middle of the road, but it's late – there are no cars. I pull my knees into my chest and rock slowly. I am crumbling. There is nothing to hold me together, not any more. Did Mum look at me and see the devil? I was her boy. That's who I was. But now ... now I am something else. Now there is nothing good in me, nothing at all.

I rock, back and forth. If I rock hard enough, I will cease to exist. If I rock hard enough, everything will stop.

That is how the man finds me – the man from the coffee shop, the man from outside the school. He crouches next to me. His name is Douglas, he tells me, although only in this life. Returners have no given names; they track each other across time by feeling their presence. They don't need to be labelled. There is no gender. Returners can come back male, female, rich, poor. It is their soul that is the same. It is their soul that the others look for.

He tells me this softly, gently, as I rock forward and back. I listen as though I am eavesdropping on someone else's conversation. He puts his arms around me; I shake them off.

'Get away from me. I don't want your sympathy. I don't deserve it. You know what I am.'

I hate him for knowing, for not kicking me when I'm down.

'It's natural to hate yourself,' he says.

'You didn't tell me,' I say, my eyes shut now. If I cannot see, I am nearer to oblivion, closer to not existing at all. 'You didn't tell me the truth.'

'The truth?'

'About who I am.'

Douglas digests this. 'You had to remember,' he says eventually.

'You said I was away for fifty years because I'd suffered. Not because . . .' I grapple for the right words. For any words. Words aren't up to the job, though. 'Not because I did that . . . I was the person who . . . who . . .'

'People suffer in different ways, Will,' Douglas says. 'You suffered terribly.'

'I killed her. I killed her baby.'

He nods. 'You did what you did. What you had to do. What you were there to do.'

'I exist to be evil?' I ask angrily. 'You think that's OK?'

'You are who you are.'

I turn this over for a few seconds. 'Am I? I didn't want to come back. I should have been there, shouldn't I? In Rwanda? The man in the van, that was supposed to be me. Killing those people. Locking the doors and waiting for them to die. But it wasn't me. It was some other Returner. I wouldn't go back.'

'You are who you are,' Douglas says again. 'Your soul needed to rest. But that does not change your destiny.'

'You should have told me the truth.' I want to be sick, want to empty out my insides, leaving a hollow shell for someone else to inhabit. Someone who isn't me.

'You weren't ready for it,' he says. 'You had to get there in your own time.'

'Get there?' My voice is sarcastic, icy. 'Oh, I got there all right.'

Douglas sits down next to me. 'You are not evil. You simply occupy human evilness. You absorb the evil just as we absorb the pain and suffering. You remember, like us.'

'I remember killing people. I remember watching people queue up as those first in line were gassed to death and burnt. I remember . . .' I can feel my nails digging into my palms. 'I've been bullying a boy at school. Every day. Punching him senseless for money. I didn't know . . .' I cannot finish the sentence. He's right. I am who I am. I didn't come back for over fifty years, but I am back now, and I am evil. I have not changed.

'Yes, you are back,' he says. I can hear the relief in his voice.

'I want to be dead.'

The thought has been in my head since I woke up; only now does it find words.

'No, Will. You don't want that.'

I don't answer.

'You suffered trauma. That's why you were away for so long.'

'*I* suffered trauma?' I can't accept it. I pull away. 'I wasn't the one who suffered. Don't you understand that?'

'I understand, Will. You will too, eventually. We all have a role to play. Each relies on the other. Each is an important part of the jigsaw.'

I stand up. 'A jigsaw? That's what you think this is?' My face is filled with disgust. 'This isn't role play. Role play is make-believe and this . . . This is very far from make-believe. Don't you understand? If I don't kill people, if I don't torture them, they don't suffer. You don't suffer. Nor do the others. It ends. It's over.' I'm staring at him, looking for a reaction, but he doesn't give me one. What did I expect? 'It's almost as if you want people to feel pain. It's almost as if you enjoy this,' I say accusingly.

Douglas smiles. It just makes me more angry. 'This isn't a game,' I say.

'No, not a joke. I'm not smiling because this isn't serious, Will. I'm smiling because you and I . . . we have discussed these things many times before. Usually we are arguing the other way round.'

I regard him stonily. 'We have not,' I say. 'You have, with someone, some other person, but not me. Not with Will Hodges.'

'No,' Douglas concedes. 'Not with Will Hodges.'

He stands up and walks towards me. 'What you are facing is the reality of human existence,' he says softly. 'The human condition. Great joy is tempered by great pain, good deeds by terrible ones. All predetermined, all set out like milestones on a journey we haven't yet made.'

'A journey I'm not going to make,' I say through gritted teeth.

'A journey that is inevitable, Will. A path that you must go down.'

I turn and stare at him. 'That's it? That's all you've got to say? You've lived a million lives and still you think this is just the way things are?'

'I have lived many lives,' Douglas agrees. 'As have you. That does not make me an expert. But it does make me understand that this is the way things are, Will.'

'Then you're as bad as me,' I say angrily. 'You're part of it. You just sit there passively and let stuff happen to you. You're complicit. I mean, what's the point? What's the point of remembering if it just happens again and again? What is the point of you? Of all the Returners? I mean, you don't fight, you don't even try to stop the evil, do you? You just let it happen. You're pathetic. You're pointless.'

Douglas takes a deep breath, then lets it out slowly. 'You're right,' he says eventually. 'You're right in some ways. We *are* passive, Will. Returners cannot change humankind. We can only inhabit the souls of humans, to absorb their pain, to remember it. Only humans themselves can fight their enemy, fight their instincts. We can only be there for them, a hand on their shoulder, by their side on their journey. We can stand in front of them and take the blow; we can protect them from themselves and inflict the agony. But we cannot change them. Only humans can change themselves.'

'And me? I don't take the blow. I inflict it.'

Douglas nods slowly. 'Yes, you do. But you also protect. You are not evil, Will. You inhabit the souls of men and women who turn to the dark side, who lose their morality, who are consumed with greed, with anger, with bitterness. Those who lose their humanity.'

'But why? They don't need protection.'

'They need a different sort of protection,' Douglas says gently.

'Sounds like a cop-out to me,' I say bitterly.

'It isn't for us to tell people how to live their lives, to force them to do as we think they should do.' I look up sharply; someone else is talking – someone else has joined us and I hadn't even noticed. It's the girl. The girl from the shopping centre. She walks towards me, hand outstretched. 'Will, no one can do that. We can only protect, as best we can –'

'Yeah,' I interrupt, 'I get it. We protect. We absorb.' I turn away; I can't bear to look at her, at Douglas, to see their eyes filled with pain, with passive acquiescence. 'Have any of you tried to stop me? To stop us? How many of us are there anyway – the bad guys, I mean?'

'It is not about good and bad, Will; they are two sides of the same coin.'

'Well, it's a stupid coin,' I say, walking away. 'It's a

pointless coin. It's a pointless, pointless world and I don't want anything else to do with it. Or you. Don't talk to me again, Douglas. Don't talk to me or look at me or follow me around. I'm done, OK? I'm done.'

But I'm not done. Of course I'm not – how could I be? My head, for so long like a jigsaw with hundreds of missing pieces whose absence I chose to ignore, is now flooding with memories; they crash like waves, swirling around, making me seasick, filling me with terror. With horror.

How long have I been doing this? How many people have suffered at my hands? Who brought me back – whose sick idea was it to create me in the first place?

And of all the memories, amongst all the horror, there is one image that brings sweat to my forehead, dries my throat to a desert. Yan's brother.

Because he is now. Because he is real. Because what has happened to him did not happen a long time ago. Because what attacked him was not another soul. It was mine. All this time I didn't get the look he was giving me. Reproach. Fear.

It was me attacking him. My hand. My fist.

Have I chosen not to remember? Do I have such a choice? Is it easier that way?

I'm feeling sick, nauseous – I don't know if it's the whisky or the knowledge of who I am that's doing it.

A car drives past and narrowly misses me; for a moment I'm sorry it didn't hit me full on.

I didn't ask for this.

Nor did the people I gassed to death. Nor did the people I tortured.

This isn't who I am.

But I know that's not true. I'm a freak. An evil, sadistic freak.

I put my hand in my pocket. Five pounds. Does he bring it every day? I wonder where he gets the money. Does his father know about it? Does Yan?

Does Claire?

The thought hits my stomach with a thud.

I have to see her. I have to explain.

The world works in strange ways. It was a deceit that led to one of my happiest memories of me and Mum. Funny, Mum hadn't ever seemed like someone who would lie; she was too pure for that, too pretty and fragrant and nice. I probably didn't even know the word deceit back then but I knew immediately that's what it was when I came home early from a friend's house one day. When I opened the door, Yan's dad was in our kitchen. With my mum. They didn't hear me come in. They were talking and drinking tea. At least, there was tea on the table. They weren't holding their mugs. They were talking intently, their heads close together.

'He doesn't know,' I heard her say. 'He can't know.'

'You have to tell him,' Yan's dad said. 'How can you love a man like that? How can you?'

She shook her head. 'Don't say that. Don't ask me that. If he thinks . . . If he finds out . . . I can't. Let me do this my way.'

Yan's dad shrugged. I stared at him, my heart thudding in my chest. We weren't meant to talk to Yan's dad, or to Yan, or his brother or any of his family by that point. Dad had told us not to. We weren't supposed to even look at them in the street. They were the lowest of the low. They'd get their comeuppance one day and in the meantime we weren't to have anything to do with any of them.

Yan's dad saw me first; he motioned to Mum, who looked up startled.

'Will! Hello, darling!' She sounded flustered. 'Gosh, you're home early. I was just . . . We were . . .'

I don't remember what else she actually said. But I do remember that she was more attentive than usual. She helped me off with my blazer, took my school bag and took out my packed lunch things. Then she started to clean them, running the hot water tap and squirting washing liquid on to the brush before scrubbing the box inside and out. Usually she wiped it with a piece of kitchen roll just before she filled it in the morning. I watched her silently. Out of the corner of my eye I could see Yan's dad watching her too.

'You all right, Will?' he said in his thick accent. He was trying to look relaxed, but I knew he wasn't.

I nodded awkwardly. I looked at my feet.

Yan's dad stood up.

'Well, thank you for the tea, Chloe. Your mother makes very good tea,' he said, smiling at me as though everything was OK.

I nodded.

Yan's dad made his excuses and left. 'We were just having a chat,' Mum said cheerfully. Too cheerfully. She looked at me for a moment, her cheeks slightly flushed. 'No need to tell Dad, is there?'

I shook my head. I made my decision easily, but it still sat heavily on me. Best friends didn't lie to each other. Best friends who lied to each other didn't stay best friends. Everyone knew that. If Dad found out . . . I pushed the thought away. I'd heard Mum and Dad arguing late at night. I'd heard noises, crashing noises, the noises people make on television when they're fighting. Whenever I heard fighting noises, Mum would be extra cheerful the following morning. She'd wear more make-up, wear brighter clothes, as though hot pink would make everything OK again.

Mum followed me around for the next hour, helping me with my homework, feeding me biscuits, asking me about the television programme I was watching. Eventually she sighed and slumped down next to me on the sofa. She put her arms around me. 'Some people burn bridges; some people build them,' she said. 'Do you understand, Will?'

I shrugged.

'The bridges I'm talking about – they're not real

bridges. They're talking bridges. Friendly bridges. So if someone upsets you, or you upset them, you build a bridge by saying sorry. Or by listening to them. Do you see?'

I thought about it. 'I told Claire she was rubbish at football on Sunday,' I said eventually. 'But afterwards I said she was better at other things. I wanted her to still be my friend.'

Mum looked at me for a moment – she looked like she was going to cry, but instead she leant over and kissed me on the forehead. 'You're a good boy, you know that, don't you?'

'Am I?'

'Oh yes, my darling. You're *my* good boy. You're the very best boy I could have.'

I still remember the glow, remember the warmth in my stomach after she said that. Her very best boy. That's who I was – not Will, not the boy who came second from bottom in spelling tests, but my mum's very best boy.

I'm not anyone's best boy any more. I'm not good at all. I'm the opposite of good.

CHAPTER SIXTEEN

I don't coo like a pigeon this time. Torturers don't do that sort of thing, do they? I just climb right up and knock on her window. It's the dead of night – it takes her a while to wake up. Then she reaches up and pulls the curtain open. She has that sweet look of dreams – soft, warm skin that's been crumpled against a pillow, a slightly confused look in her eye. I get a sudden desperate urge to be her, to have the innocence of not knowing what's gone before and what's coming in the future. To just live life as it happens.

She frowns at me, then opens the window. 'I'm tired, Will. Is this important?'

I nod and clamber in. She yawns and falls back against the pillow. I sit at the end of her bed; I pull one of her soft, warm blankets around myself.

Claire sits up again. 'You look awful. You're shivering. You're . . . Will, what are you wearing?'

I look down – I am wearing socks that have been dirtied by the road, pyjama bottoms and a T-shirt. My socks have holes in them.

I shrug eventually. 'I was in a hurry,'

'A hurry.' She is looking at me suspiciously. 'Why? Not the dreams again?'

I nod. Then I shake my head. How can I explain? I suddenly feel very old. Very alone. Maybe it was a bad idea to come here. I don't want to infect Claire with my misery, with what I know. I don't want her to turn on me, and yet I'd be disappointed if she didn't.

'Will? Tell me. Tell me what's up.'

'It's kind of the dreams, but worse than that,' I say carefully. 'I had them again, but they're not dreams. They're who I am. I'm one of them. One of the Returners. Not even one of them. I'm evil, Claire. I'm the devil. I saw myself. I saw who I am. They were real, Claire. They happened. I was there. I was there . . .'

The tears that would not come before are streaming now. Self-pity? I despise myself even as I cry. Claire puts her arms around me; I pull away.

'I don't deserve your sympathy,' I manage to say. 'I want you to hate me. I want you to despise everything about me.'

I realise I mean it – it would make me feel better. My revulsion with myself is not enough.

'OK.' She's teasing me – I can tell from her eyes.

'I'm not joking. This is serious, Claire. You have no idea how serious.'

And suddenly I am afraid. Afraid I might hurt her, like I've hurt others. I edge backwards. 'I should go.'

'Will.' She folds her arms irritably. 'You've woken me up. At least have the decency to tell me why.'

I swallow. My throat is parched. My eyes fall on a glass of water on Claire's bedside table. She follows my gaze and hands it to me. I drink it immediately; the water is cool and soothing. I don't deserve it.

I take a deep breath. 'The people,' I say. 'The people who've been following me. The Returners. They lied to me.'

'Of course they were lying,' Claire says, rolling her eyes. 'OK, Will. Look, I know things aren't easy for you at the moment, but come on. There's no such thing as a Returner. I don't know who these people are, but they are just one big lie; they really are. You have to tell someone about them. Maybe . . .' She frowns, her brow creasing gently. 'Have you thought about going back to that doctor?'

My eyes narrow. 'You mean the shrink?'

'Doctor,' she corrects me. 'He was nice, wasn't he?'

I don't say anything for a moment or two. The disappointment is too great, like the plug has been pulled out and I'm running down the plughole. She thinks I'm mad. I thought she understood. I thought we were friends again.

I have no friends.

I have no one.

I steady myself. I concentrate. I breathe slowly. I allow my blood to freeze; that way I am safe.

'Interesting theory,' I say, a new edge to my voice, ignoring her comment about the shrink, 'but you're wrong. They do exist. They are Returners and I'm one of them. Only I'm not. I'm different.'

'What do you mean different?'

'I'm the bad guy.' I say it flatly, no emotion. It sounds like I'm talking about a film.

Claire raises an eyebrow. 'The bad guy?'

'I'm the devil.' It's strange – it feels almost as if I am showing off. As though I am proud of this fact.

Claire looks at me curiously, then sees that I'm serious, that I'm not smiling. She opens her mouth, then closes it again. A few seconds go by; they seem to last for ever.

'The devil?' she asks eventually. 'What do you mean exactly?'

'I mean,' I say, 'that I'm the one who causes suffering, not the one who suffers. My dreams . . . they aren't dreams. They're memories. I remember now. I have killed people. I have tortured people. I am the devil.'

I feel strangely calm.

'You kill?' Claire looks at me sceptically.

'The lines of people,' I say quietly, as though I'm talking about something utterly mundane. Detachment. Complete detachment. It is not me, it does not matter, it is nothing. They are nothing. Everything is nothing.

'I could smell the ash. And I thought I was with them, one of them. I thought that's what it was. But I wasn't. I was the . . .'

187

Her eyes are on me, staring. They make me feel uncomfortable. 'The ash? What ash? What lines?'

'At the camp. I was at Auschwitz. I wasn't a prisoner, Claire.'

'You weren't?' She looks scared now. It's sinking in. She will understand soon. She won't be able to look me in the eye. It will make what I have to do easier.

'Yan's brother,' I say. 'I've been stealing his money. I didn't know I was doing it, but every day I've been beating him up and taking a fiver from him. Every day.'

'You're the one who's been beating up Yan's brother?'

I nod.

Her eyes are wide, clouded. She is trying to make sense of the nonsensical.

'That's you? You've been doing that to him?' She is incredulous. She is outraged. 'It's not enough that bigots have been scrawling graffiti on their house, putting bricks through their windows? You've been beating up that poor boy? You?'

I nod. It feels strangely cathartic to confess. I need her judgement, need her to hate me.

'And you really don't remember?'

'I do now.'

'The whole family have been so worried,' Claire says. 'They tried telling the school but no one listens to them.' She shakes her head bitterly. 'Because they're immigrants.'

She lets the word hang in the air for a few seconds. Then she rounds on me again. 'He . . . won't talk about it. They tried not giving him money but the . . . you, I mean . . . It made it worse. He came home with a broken nose.'

She isn't talking to me; she is talking to herself. She edges backwards, catches me looking at her and flushes. Then she stands up, goes on the offensive, to hide her embarrassment. I can see it all now, can see every reason for every action. How? Because I have seen it all before? Because I have lived so many lives?

'And it was you all along? Jesus, Will. Do you know what it's done to him? To the family?'

'No. Anyway, I came to say goodbye.'

'Goodbye?'

'I'm going away. I wanted you to say sorry. To Yan's brother.'

Claire looks angry. 'Tell him yourself tomorrow. Don't run away, Will. Face up to it.'

'No,' I say. 'No.'

'You can't just run away from what you've done. You think that'll make it OK? It won't. You have to make amends. You have to face up to what you've done, pay the price.'

'No, Claire,' I say, a shade of anger slipping into my voice. 'There's another thing. Before I go.'

'Yes?' Her voice has lost any trace of warmth, of friendship. It is as though the sun has gone in. I shiver.

'Yan,' I say. 'He didn't do it.'

'I know. Everyone knows. Everyone except . . .' She

stops herself just in time from mentioning my father and Patrick.

'They planted evidence,' I say. 'A knife. To make it look as though it was him. I heard them talking about it.'

'Heard who?' Claire gasps.

'Dad and Patrick.'

'Oh my God.'

'Yeah. Well, anyway, now you know.'

'But that's not enough. You have to tell someone official. You have to say that in court. You have to.'

'I can't,' I say. 'I have to go. I've done all I can, OK?'

I clamber on the bed and open the window.

'You haven't done all you can. Yan's still in prison.' Her bottom lip is sticking out, like it used to when she was younger and having a hissy fit because she wasn't getting her way. On impulse I lean forward and kiss her, right on the mouth. She is soft. She is warm. For a second I feel complete, I feel like a person, like there are other possibilities, another way . . .

But there is no other way. I know that.

'Bye, Claire,' I say. She says nothing – she is too surprised to speak. I haul myself out of her window and clamber down the wall.

CHAPTER SEVENTEEN

It's not late any more – it's early. Very early. The sky and the water are beautiful; it's like they're both reflected in each other. Both bright, light, shimmering. Both full of the hope and optimism of newness, of fresh starts.

I wrap my arms around myself – it's chilly, the kind of chilly that suggests that it's going to be a hot day, that there are no clouds hanging around to spoil things.

A day I won't see.

A day I won't enjoy.

I wouldn't enjoy it anyway, I remind myself. Does evil enjoy itself? Can it?

I stare at the river, deep into it. I'm at the same spot, the exact same position I was in when my mother . . . drowned herself . . .

I wish she was here – wish she was sitting right

next to me, to guide me, to help me.

I don't know what to do, Mum.

Yes, I do. I know exactly what to do. It's just . . . I'm scared.

I see two figures walking towards me – they're still a way away, but I recognise them. I look away – I'm ashamed at the relief coursing through me. Because as long as they're here, I won't be able to do it. And yet I also feel afraid, in case they try to stop me. Will I be strong enough to resist? Will I be brave enough?

I hear them getting closer. I still don't turn around, even when Douglas sits down next to me on the bench. The girl sits on my other side.

'Will,' Douglas says by way of a greeting. 'We thought we might find you here.'

'Yeah?' I stretch my legs out. I don't want to touch either of them.

'It's not the answer, Will. You can't run away.'

'I'm not running away,' I say angrily. 'I'm taking control.'

'No, Will. Returners can't take control. What you're doing is fighting, resisting. You shouldn't. You'll only get hurt.' It's the girl talking. I turn to look at her, at her haunting eyes, her pale skin and slight frame. She looks so fragile. I wonder what she remembers, what she has seen.

But she's wrong. She has to be.

'No,' I say simply. 'You're wrong.'

'She's right,' Douglas says soberly. 'You don't have control. No one does. Humans don't control where they are born, to whom, into which century. Returners don't have control either. You can't change what you are, Will. You can try to run but you'll still be you. You'll come back somewhere else. Accept your destiny, don't fight it.'

'Don't fight it? Easy for you to say.'

I turn, momentarily, and see his eyes. His sad eyes. I hang my head.

'I didn't mean that,' I say. 'I know it's not easy for you.' I look at him searchingly, then at the girl. 'You haven't told me where you've been, what you've been through.'

Douglas smiles. 'We would be here for days if we told you everything.'

'Edited highlights then,' I say. 'Lowlights, I mean,' then feel guilty for making a joke of it.

'Only when you've stared suffering in the face can you laugh at it,' he says, reading my mind, or guessing really well. He winks at me. 'Never be afraid to laugh at anything – black humour is one of humankind's survival mechanisms. Without it we really are in trouble. Doctors are renowned for their grim humour – surgeons are the worst.'

I feel myself smiling back. A half-smile anyway. It's strange – how can someone who's only ever suffered be so comfortable to be with?

I sit back, pull my knees into my chest. 'So tell me.'

Douglas leans into the bench. 'We'll tell you,' he says. 'So long as you promise not to do anything stupid.'

'I promise,' I say.

'OK then. Let's see. What do you know about India?'

I shrug. 'Not much.'

'Well, you should,' he says. 'India is a beautiful, rich continent, full of some of the most vibrant people in the world.'

'You were there?'

'Several times.'

'And?'

He smiles and shrugs. 'The wars when the colonialists left – they were brutal. I was raped several times –'

'Raped?' I look at him in horror.

'As a woman,' he says. 'I have lived as woman and man. So have you. In that life all my children were killed in front of me, all of us were left to die.'

I think of something that makes my hair stand on end. 'Was I there? Was I one of the –'

Douglas shakes his head. 'Not then. But our paths have crossed, Will, many times. As I'm sure they will again.'

'And you don't hate me? You don't want to hit me? To kill me?'

The girl's hand moves to my arm. 'Will, it's not like that.'

'No?' I round on her. 'Then what is it like? Please explain, because to be honest I really don't get it. I mean, I'm an evil bastard, right? And you've endured horror and pain in all your thousands of lives or however many there have been. And yet you're here with me like we're old friends.'

Douglas lets out a sigh. 'You know,' he says, 'after a war, soldiers find it hard to talk to civilians about what they've been through. They often become recluses; marriages break up and old friendships are torn apart. Ex-combatants can often only talk to each other because only then do they know that they are understood, that they aren't being judged, that they can be themselves. Soldiers on the other side, the enemy, understand better what a soldier has been through than his own wife.'

'We're all soldiers together?' I look at him incredulously. 'That's rubbish. I'm the soldier; you're the civilians back home who've been bombed to smithereens.'

Douglas clears his throat. 'OK, how's your history, Will?'

I shrug. 'Not great,' I say testily.

'You know about the First World War?'

'Some.'

'Have you heard about the armistice? The Christmas armistice?'

I shake my head.

'Ah,' Douglas says. 'Well, let me tell you what happened. It was 1914, December 24th. The trenches were a grim affair. You've heard of them, I suppose?'

I roll my eyes. 'Sure. Mud and stuff.'

'Mud, ice, dead bodies, lack of sanitation, yes,'

Douglas says gravely. 'And then on Christmas Eve there was a ceasefire. It wasn't organised or anything. It was just Christmas. And the Germans didn't want to fight any more than the British or the French or the Belgians. They sent notes over asking for a ceasefire. They gave each other cigarettes, chocolate cake. They sang carols and celebrated Christmas. They even played football.'

'Seriously?' I frown. 'You're not making this up?'

'I'm not making it up, no,' Douglas confirms.

'OK,' I say dubiously. 'But what has that got to do with me?'

'Don't you see?' Douglas looks at me carefully. 'We are soldiers on different sides of the same battle. We are here because of each other. And there is no fighting at the moment. We are at peace.'

I think about this for a while. 'And the next day?' I say eventually. 'What happened when it was all over?'

'When it was all over?' Douglas looks at the girl, who squeezes my arm.

'Then it was back to war,' she says. 'They started fighting again.'

'Right,' I say uncomfortably. 'So it didn't mean anything.'

'It meant everything,' Douglas says. 'The dividing lines were not between people. They rarely are. They are between political stances, ideologies, beliefs.'

I look out over the river. I feel confused, uncertain. I turn to the girl. 'Was I there? During the First World War. I don't remember it.'

She looks over at Douglas, who nods. 'You weren't there,' she says. 'You died in the Mexican Revolution.'

'The Mexican Revolution.' Images flash into my mind – of heat, of power, of attackers. 'I was attacked.' I look at Douglas hopefully. 'I was attacked. Me. I wasn't the one who . . . I mean, they killed me. I remember it.'

'After you massacred anyone who rebelled against you,' Douglas says wryly. 'You ruled the place for thirty-four years before you were deposed.'

My shoulders slump. 'Right. Yeah,' I say. I sigh. 'So anyway, you were telling me about India.'

Douglas frowns. 'Will, I can tell you, but the stories are all the same. India, Africa, right here in the UK. There's Mongolia, six hundred years ago – I was beheaded as part of an ethnic cleansing exercise. Russia, forty years ago – I was sent to Siberia, to a work camp, died of hypothermia. Hungary, five hundred years ago – stoned to death as the Ottoman Empire spread into my country. Humans may progress, Will. They may think that they are moving forward because they have invented clever machines and because they control the land and sea. But man's capacity to inflict and endure pain is constant. Man's desire for power, to beat down his competition – it hasn't changed in the slightest.'

The girl nods. 'The stories don't matter,' she says. 'They're all the same in their different ways.'

'All the same.' I repeat her words. Something is bugging me, but I'm not sure what. And then I realise

197

what it is. I stand up. I want to be looking at both of them. 'So what's the point?'

'The point?' Douglas frowns.

'You said that Returners exist to absorb the pain, to remember it for humankind.'

'That's right.'

'But what's the point, if people carry on doing terrible things, if I keep coming back, and others like me, to inflict more suffering? What do you achieve?'

He smiles sadly. 'We can't change humankind,' he says. 'Human nature is what it is. Driven by desire for material things, for love, for conquest, for knowledge. The best and the worst come out of this desire.'

'But if history just keeps repeating itself, then why remember? When it doesn't do any good? I mean, people are always rewriting history. And what's the point of remembering if you don't remind people once in a while?'

The girl looks at me sadly. 'Memories don't have to be at the forefront of the mind to exist, Will.'

'But nothing ever changes.'

'It does. It just happens slowly.'

'So what happened in Auschwitz will never happen again?'

She looks uncomfortable. 'It's not like that,' she says.

'Then what is it like?'

'You are asking the wrong questions, looking at this the wrong way. What Emily is trying to explain is that our paths are all set,' Douglas says gently.

'Emily?' My head swings round to look at the girl. I realise I didn't even know her name.

'Names don't matter,' she says, reading my mind.

'Nothing seems to matter to you,' I say bitterly. 'Not the fact that I don't know your name, not the fact that some people kill other people, not the fact that some people torture and maim other people. But it does matter. It all matters.'

'It matters, but not in the way you think,' she says. 'We are comrades throughout time. Names are transient.'

'Maybe to you,' I say staunchly. 'Maybe you're beyond names. But I'm not. I'm Will Hodges. And I am not going to do this. I'm not going to do whatever it is you think I'm going to.'

'We don't know what you're going to do,' Douglas says. 'But it is not for you to choose.'

'You mean my choice has been made for me? No. No way.'

'Not made for you, no. But we will always make the same choices. We are who we are.'

I shake my head. 'I refuse to be who you say I am.'

He stands up and takes my hand. Emily takes the other one; I feel warm suddenly, as though I have just come in from the cold. 'I don't think I have explained it very well,' Douglas continues. 'Returners hold on to humanity's violent secrets out of love, out of hope.'

'Hope?' The word makes me feel uncomfortable. *Her eyes, looking at me. Begging me. Hopeful.*

'How can you feel hope when you know your life is

doomed to be full of suffering?'

'We need hope and love, Will. Without either of those . . . well, that's when the suffering will start in earnest. That's when everything will come to an end.'

'And returning brings hope?' My voice is heavy with sarcasm.

'Absorbing the pain stops hope from being destroyed.'

'Hope gets destroyed,' I say bitterly. 'Trust me.'

Douglas looks at me sadly. 'Tell me, Will, is there love in your life? Is there hope?'

I think of Claire. Think of Dad. I think of Mum.

But she's gone. They've all gone. It's just me on my own. I have to deal with this, take control. I am in shade, I am in scrubland, I am in a swamp, I am sinking. I feel myself getting angry. I am resentful. I feel pain and it hurts and I want it to go away, and it is Douglas's fault, I see that suddenly. He is making me feel bad and I want him to go, want them both to go, and yet they are still here.

'Go,' I bark.

Douglas shakes his head. 'We won't leave you, Will. We know what you intend to do, and we won't let you do it. It will only cause you more pain. You have run away for long enough; you need to accept things as they are.'

'I'll do what I want,' I say. The anger is rising up like a tsunami, quick and deadly.

'Of course you will. But allow us to guide you at least.'

'Guide me? Guide me?' I am furious. I feel rage coursing through my veins. I grab him, I throw him to the ground. He doesn't resist. I kick him. He lets me. It makes me more angry, more bitter. He is pathetic. I am strong and he is weak and he will *learn*, he must *learn* . . . I throw myself down on the ground on top of him; I am hitting him, grabbing him by the neck. My hands hurt; it feels good. It feels as though I am wresting control, as though I am in charge. I am just doing to him what he wants me to do, what he expects me to do. He is responsible for this, and he must pay. He must pay.

Suddenly I stop. My anger has evaporated; I can't remember its source any more. I get to my knees and I stare at my hands in horror. What have I done? What just happened? I feel hands on my shoulders – Emily's hands. I shake her off. 'Don't touch me.'

'It's OK, Will,' Douglas says, pulling himself up painfully. His cheek is bleeding, his voice is strangled. 'It's OK.'

'It's OK,' Emily echoes. She is standing next to Douglas now. Their haunted eyes are fixed on me.

'You are who you are,' they say in unison.

'What am I?' I whisper. My hands are bruised. A lump is appearing above Douglas's eye. I look away. 'I don't know why I did that.'

'Yes, you do. You were angry. You blame me for that anger.'

He's right, but I won't admit it. Can't admit it. 'You didn't even try and stop me. You didn't fight back.'

'Returners don't fight back. It is not for us to stop what happens. We are what we are, Will. We all play our role.'

He is smiling; I look at him incredulously. I hate him for smiling. Hate him for telling me I cannot change. 'If you won't help yourself, then *I'll* help you,' I say, 'and you can't stop me.'

I stand up and walk towards the water's edge. I am full of self-loathing. I am evil. There is nothing else I can do to stop it.

'That isn't the answer and you know it,' Emily says.

'Think, Will. Think of the people you love. Think of your hopes, their hopes. You are part of those hopes. The fabrics of your lives intertwine. You belong here, you must live your life as it is intended to be lived. Running away will not help you or anyone else.'

'Living won't help anyone if I'm evil,' I say, my voice choked.

'Evil is an emotive word,' Douglas says. 'Unhelpful too. You are yin to our yang. You have a different energy force, that's all.'

'Like Hitler did?' I swing round and stare at them defiantly.

'History moves along a certain course,' Douglas says gently. 'One cannot fight it. Be with the people you love. Be who you are. Make peace with your destiny.'

I move away from the water, sit back down on the bench, let my head drop into my hands.

And suddenly I am crying. Weeping. I don't even

know why. Is it shame? Or is it fear?

Emily sits beside me; Douglas stands over me. We stay like that for a few minutes. Then I wipe my eyes. As I do so, something hits me. Something important. Something I've been pushing from my head. 'Dad,' I say. The conversation with Patrick. He's doing something wrong. Something terrible. He doesn't realise, doesn't see. And Yan. He didn't do it. He shouldn't be in prison.

'You love your father,' Douglas says. 'And he needs you.'

I shake my head. Then I nod. I think of Dad's face, of his sitting in the chair alone, always alone since Mum died. 'He doesn't need me.' My voice has gone all raspy. I wasn't even going to say goodbye to him. I was just going to leave him. Like Mum did. Only this time he'd have had no one. No one at all.

'What is it, Will? Tell me.'

'I won't be . . . I can't be who you say I am,' I manage to say.

'Perhaps not now. But it's who you are, Will. It's who you will become.'

'No.'

Douglas stands up. 'You promised you wouldn't do anything stupid, remember.'

'Killing a future murderer isn't stupid in my book,' I say, even though I already know I can't do it, can't do what Mum did.

'You know we're here for you,' Douglas says, turning and starting to walk. Emily gives me one last look, a smile framed by mournful eyes, then walks after him.

It's properly light now; I realise they have cleverly kept me talking until daylight. There's a woman on the other side of the river walking her dog; there will be other people soon. It is too late.

I stand up and let the early rays of the new day's sun warm my face, warm my bones. I have goose-bumps; I need to eat, to have a hot shower.

I hear something, footsteps, quiet ones, creeping ones, from behind me, from behind the bushes, and I swing round, then stop, my mouth falling open.

'Will?'

It's Claire.

'Will, I'm sorry, I . . . When you said goodbye like that I was worried. Worried what you might do. I followed you. I'm sorry. I was going to just go, but . . .'

I stare at her. 'You followed me? You've been here all the time?'

'For ages.' She's shivering, her wide eyes surrounded by shadows.

'You mean you heard.'

She nods. 'They were . . . That was them?' she asks. 'Returners?'

'Yeah.'

She looks at me, right into my eyes. 'You were going to do it, weren't you? You were going to . . . in the river, I mean. Like your mum.'

'I guess.' I put my hands in my pockets awkwardly.

'That man is right. You can't run away.'

I roll my eyes. 'So what then? I just stay put and wait for whatever it is that's going to happen? Wait until it's time to kill some more people?'

'No.' She bites her lip, maintains her gaze. Her eyes are so clear, so true, so defiant. They never show any hint of doubt, of uncertainty. 'You have to fight, Will.'

'Fight, yeah. Fight and torture and –'

'Not that sort of fighting.' Her voice is growing in confidence. 'I've been thinking about it and I think that man is wrong. Nothing is set in stone, Will. Nothing is determined, not until it's happened. You don't have to be who they say you're going to be, who you think you're going to be. You can be some-one else. You can change. Everyone can. We all make our own decisions, every single day.'

I shake my head. 'Making a decision about whether to have Cheerios or Shreddies isn't the same as decid-ing whether to be an agent of evil or not,' I say. 'Look, thanks for the vote of confidence, but you don't get it. Look at what I've already done – to Yan's brother, to Dad. I'm bad. Deep down. I'm not a nice person, Claire. I'm not nice at all. I saw it all tonight. I remember it. Auschwitz – I was there. Rwanda – I was supposed to lock those people in the school . . .'

I wipe my eyes angrily.

'But that's just it, Will. You're not that person. Not really,' Claire says, looking at me intently. 'You told me about Yan, about your dad. You care. You hate the characters you inhabit in those dreams.

Nightmares, I mean. Maybe there's some Returner soul inside you that's evil, but that's not you. You can fight it. You can, I know you can.'

I want to believe her. But I know I can't. 'No.'

'You can. I'll help you.'

'Help me? How?'

'You do these things without knowing. Well, if I'm always with you, you'll know. I mean, I'll stop you.'

I raise an eyebrow. 'You'll stop me?'

'Yes.' She folds her arms.

'What if I hurt you? What if I turn on you, like I turned on Yan's brother? What then?'

Claire shrugs. We're walking back towards town. 'You won't.'

'I might.'

'No.' She looks up at me, bites her lip. 'You remember why we stopped being friends?'

I look at her awkwardly. 'I guess you found better people to hang out with.'

'No, Will. That's not what happened.'

'It isn't? So what? We just drifted apart then?'

'No,' she says again. I feel my stomach clench. Another chunk missing from my life. What did I do? What did I do to her?

'It was your dad.'

'Dad?' I frown. 'What are you talking about?'

'My parents took Yan's family's side. In their argument with your dad. He told you not to be friends with me any more.'

'He did?' I don't remember any of this. 'And I just

stopped being friends with you? Just like that?'

She shakes her head. 'No, you didn't. That's the point. You were really brave. You told him that we were friends and he couldn't do anything about it. You said that his fight with Yan's dad had nothing to do with me. Or you.'

'Right.' I'm confused. 'So . . . why did we . . . ?'

'He threatened me,' she says quietly. 'He shouted at me, told me I was an immigrant-lover. Said I should be careful.'

'Dad said that?' I feel myself stiffen with anger.

'He'd been drinking. You said he didn't know what he was saying.' She takes my hand. 'You said we should stop being friends. Stop seeing each other.'

'I said that?' I ask incredulously.

'You wanted to protect me. You were worried for me. You said you'd be fine, that it would be better this way.'

'I said that.' This time it isn't a question. I can sort of remember, maybe, in a hazy kind of way, like it happened a lifetime ago.

'You definitely did. I remember,' Claire says. 'You're a good person, Will. I know you are. And you'd never hurt me. So now it's my turn to look after you. OK?'

She squeezes my hand and I want to believe her. I do believe her. I'm Will Hodges. I'm a good person. And Claire is going to be with me all the time. I will never be alone again. 'OK,' I whisper, as we walk back home. 'If you say so.'

CHAPTER EIGHTEEN

I get back home to find Dad in the sitting room waiting for me. Patrick is with him, grim-faced.

Patrick rushes over to me, grabs me. 'Where the hell have you been? Your dad has been up all night worrying about you. What d'you think you're playing at? Who've you been with?'

I look at him curiously. 'Why should you care?'

He looks like he wants to hit me. Dad is on his chair. He has a black eye. He looks at me warily. An image flashes into my mind: Dad on the floor, his nose bloody. I feel a shudder of guilt.

I did that.

I punched my own father.

'I don't care about you, you little shit,' Patrick says. It is as though a veil has lifted. This is the real Patrick. The smiles, the jokes, they were all a charade. 'But I do care about your dad. About justice.'

Justice. OK, now I get it. I say nothing; just look at him blankly, baiting him.

'So come on. Where have you been?'

'Out,' I say.

His face is going red. If Dad weren't here, he would not be restraining himself.

'Out where?' This time it's Dad talking. I look at him.

'I'm sorry,' I say. 'I didn't mean to worry you.'

'Didn't mean to worry him? Out all night? Don't make me laugh,' Patrick says sarcastically.

'I didn't,' I say levelly. 'I just needed some fresh air.'

'You've got a garden, haven't you?' Patrick interjects. I choose to ignore him.

'You were with that Hayes girl,' Dad says. 'You know I don't want you hanging around that family? I thought we understood each other.'

'Claire?' My eyes narrow just slightly. 'I wasn't with her,' I lie.

'Funny that. I saw the two of you together just a few minutes ago.' Patrick is smiling smugly. 'Thought I'd take a drive, see if I could track you down.'

I regard him stonily. I cannot let him see that I am concerned for her. 'I wasn't with her. I just bumped into her. I couldn't care less about Claire Hayes. I went for a walk, OK? On my own. To let off some steam.'

Patrick's not sure what to say, not sure whether I'm having a laugh at him or being genuine. He looks at Dad, who shrugs.

'You say anything to her?' Patrick's gaze returns to me.

'About what?'

'You know her parents are troublemakers? You know they'd rather see foreigners living off our taxes than English people born and bred doing the jobs that are theirs by rights?'

I don't say anything. Patrick moves towards me threateningly. 'Did you say anything to her,' he asks again, enunciating each syllable. 'About the boy. The foreign boy.'

'About Yan?' I ask. 'He has a name.'

'Don't you . . .' Patrick moves towards me but I don't flinch. He catches Dad's eye and checks himself. 'You're not worth it anyway,' he says. 'Soon you'll be a long way away, out of trouble, Will,' he says. 'Your dad's found you a new school.'

'A new school?' I look at him uncertainly.

'It's a boarding school. More like a camp. They teach kids like you some respect.' He grins. 'Ooh, Will, just you wait. Ooh, you're in for a treat.'

'I don't want to go away to school,' I say to Dad. 'I like my school.' I'd normally smile at the irony of that statement, but right now I'm not really in the mood to smile. Dad isn't looking at me. It's like he's barely there, like he's already bailed out.

'Your dad doesn't want a smart-arse son who thinks he knows better than everyone,' Patrick says. 'You're going to learn some discipline. The people who run the school, they're friends of mine. They know what they're doing. They won't take any shit from you. They'll make you into a man, Will.'

'A man?' An image flashes into my mind. A speech I am giving. *You are the sons of Great Britain. You will make our country great again. You will lead others, lead them to a bright and honourable future. You will reclaim our country* ... 'Like you, you mean?'

I watch Patrick go red.

'What are you saying, Will?' he asks. 'Just what are you saying, you freak? You friendless, guileless freak? You're going to turn into your mother if you're not careful. You hear me? You're pathetic. You're a loser, Will.'

He's angry. But not as angry as me. It fills my veins, my arteries, hot and red; then I turn a switch and it is cool blue. Angry blue. Icy.

'Well, you know about being a loser,' I say. 'You can't catch a murderer so you fit someone else up. You're the one who's pathetic.'

He's staring at me, his mouth open. 'What did you just say?'

'I said you're pathetic. I said that I know what you did. What you're doing with Yan. Fitting him up. Smart, Patrick. Really smart. What do you think people will say when they find out? When I tell them the truth? Because I'm going to. I'm going to tell them everything, and you're going to be ruined. No career, no poxy job title to make you feel like a big man. You'll be nothing. You'll be worse than nothing.'

'You little . . .' Patrick lunges at me. 'How dare you, you little shit? How dare you?'

I'm ready for him. My fist is clenched, my body taut. Dad looks at me, then at Patrick. He is shocked. He is not prepared for this. I wait for him to help me.

'Get over here,' Patrick barks.

He stands up just as Patrick pulls me to the floor. My dad is not going to help me. The two of them pin me down. Dad averts his eyes.

'Is that what you've been talking about with that little slut Claire Hayes?' Patrick asks through gritted teeth. His eyes are bloodshot, his face bulbous and covered in thin red veins. 'She been asking you about the foreign boy, has she? You know why?'

He is pushing down on my chest; I can barely breathe. I refuse to look at him; I turn my head.

'I'll tell you why.' He laughs. 'You think she cares about you, don't you? She doesn't give a shit. She's only looking out for her *boyfriend*.'

I try to pull away, but Dad and Patrick are holding me down too tight.

'You don't know what you're talking about,' I say instead. I hear Claire's voice telling me I am a good person, telling me she will always be with me.

'She's been down to the prison every day to see him,' Patrick says, grinning. He's clearly enjoying himself. 'Kissing him, bringing him things. Shame – nice English girl like her.'

'No.'

'She's just like her parents, Will. Selfish. Manipu-

212

lative. She's the enemy, Will, and you can't even see it.'

I close my eyes to block him out. But a flash of images fills my mind. *Checkpoints, walls being built. Claire on one side. Come over, Claire. Come with me. She's shaking her head. She's going with him. With Yan. She's choosing him . . .*

I open my eyes to see him holding some tape. He hands it to Dad and gets a better grip on my hands. My stomach drops down into the pit of my belly when I realise it's for me. They're tying me up. I wrestle, I writhe, but it's no good. They tape my hands behind my back.

'It's for your own good, son,' Dad says. 'You'll see that eventually. You'll thank me one day.'

One day. I know the day he talks of. I can see it. *The checkpoints are closing. The gates are coming down. England for the English. Safety within our borders. I am saluting. The crowds are cheering. Behind them the cast-offs, stuffed into ships, crammed into corners, are disappearing. Not our problem any more. Not our problem . . .*

I want the images to go away. I open my eyes, see my father's empty ones, close mine again. I struggle. My head is pounding. I start to scream. 'Let me go. Let me go.'

'Drink this, son.'

Liquid forced into my mouth; I gag, but swallow most of it.

I can hear their screams. I can see Claire's face,

looking at me with disgust. She is with them. 'This isn't my country any more,' she is saying. 'I want nothing more to do with it. Nothing more to do with you.'

'Please, Claire,' I shout.

'Pathetic,' Patrick says again. 'Will, the girl's been using you. She's shagging the foreign boy.' His face takes on a look of distaste when he says 'foreign' – to him it is an insult, not a description.

His voice sounds funny, like someone's slowed it down. I can't open my eyes; don't want to. I'm tired. I'm heavy.

I hear Dad sigh. 'Jeez, I thought he'd never stop.'

'Yeah,' Patrick says. 'Like you said before, takes after his mother.'

CHAPTER NINETEEN

I'm awake. At least, I think I'm awake. Something's wrong. Maybe I'm dreaming. I open my eyes. No, not dreaming. I'm in my room, on my bed. I try to move my hand and I can't. I contemplate this for a few minutes, then let it go. It seems unimportant. I'm comfortable; I just can't move my hands. No big deal. There's nothing I need to move them for right now anyway.

I try to focus, but it's like trying to hold a cloud in my hand – my mind is floating about everywhere, unable to hold a single thought for more than a nanosecond. I see images – Claire, Yan, Claire and Yan . . . I see them holding hands. I see him kissing her. It hurts like a knife in my chest. My anger flares up, but even that won't hold; it drifts away towards the horizon.

In my mind's eye, Yan's a cardboard cut-out. I flick

him and he falls over and Claire looks at me and smiles and she is mine again. That's better.

But he pops up again. Yan, I mean. He isn't a cardboard cut-out; he's a punch-ball. I can hit him as hard as I like and he just bounces back. I need a pin. I don't have a pin.

I ask Claire for one, but she just looks at me blankly and shakes her head.

The door opens. I'm not sure if I've been dreaming or daydreaming. Not sure what the difference is right now. I turn to see Dad walking in. He sits down at the end of my bed.

'You're awake then, son?'

I feel angry with him. I don't know why. But my anger soon evaporates; it's too much effort. I shut my eyes and let the feeling of floating take over. Soft and fluffy. Enveloped. Safe.

'I'm sorry about . . . earlier. But you're OK now. Everything's going to be OK, Will.'

The words go in; I contemplate them; they drift out again. He's sorry? Why? I try to remember.

'It's for the best, you see,' Dad continues. 'You'll see. You're young. You don't see what I see. You don't understand people yet. Patrick's just looking out for you, son. He's looking out for both of us. You and me, we're a team. The two of us.'

I open my eyes again to look at him; they close a few seconds later. Better that way. Drifting. My hands are uncomfortable; I think about asking Dad to untie them, but can't muster the energy. There are more important things. But what? I don't know what is important. I can't remember.

'Used to be three of us. All for one and one for all? Not as far as your mother was concerned. Patrick warned me about her, and I didn't listen. But you're not like that, are you, Will? You understand, don't you? About loyalty. About teamwork. We're on the same side, me and you. You remember that, don't you? You remember?'

I nod. *Same side*. I remember the words. We used to be on the same side. Yes, I'm sure we were. Did we stop? I see his angry face bearing down on me, I feel a surge of resentment. Why? I try to remember. I see his eyes, tired, broken. Patrick pushing me to the floor. But that was before, not now. Now there is no resentment. It feels good to be on the same side as someone. Especially Dad. I want him to like me. I feel all warm suddenly, like I'm young again. I realise why – he's stroking my head. Like Mum used to do.

He moves further on to the bed, leans against the wall with a sigh. It's raining, heavy drops pelt against the window. Safe and warm inside. I was outside. When? I try to concentrate, try to remember. The river. I was by the river.

'I was by the river,' I say, for no real reason. 'I was there. Mum. She was there . . .'

'That was a long time ago,' Dad says, quietly.

I open my mouth. I want to tell him that it wasn't, that I was there just now, just an hour ago . . . But I'm confused. Mum wasn't there. Was she?

'You know,' Dad continues, 'she wasn't herself, your mum. At the end. He'd turned her, that bastard.'

He looks at me for a few seconds, scrutinising my face. My mouth closes. So do my eyes.

'That's what they do, you see. They want to take over. That's what you've got to understand. That Yan, he's like his dad. He can't help himself – it's in their nature. They're parasites. They steal from people. His father tried to steal your mother. You can't trust foreigners, Will.'

Yan. The anger flares up again. I need a pin. I need a pin.

The cloud is slowly evaporating. I frown again. I like the cloud. I like the feeling of safety. I open my eyes again. They aren't so heavy now. I can see Dad's face properly. He looks like he's been crying. I frown. Dad doesn't cry. The cloud is slowly evaporating. I frown again. I like the cloud. I like the feeling of safety.

'The thing is, son, we have to fight them. Otherwise we're history. Otherwise we're going to lose this country, lose everything we've worked for, that our fathers have worked for. It's like Patrick says – you don't have someone to stay, then sit by while they tell you that half your house is now legally theirs, do you? It isn't right. But that's what they've done. They came here and now they're taking over.'

'Taking over,' I manage to say. 'Yan can't take Claire, Dad.'

Dad looks slightly startled at the fact that I've

spoken. 'Don't you worry about that Claire. She's not worth it, son. She's as bad as them. You'll find someone better.'

'There's no one better,' I mutter. 'Claire, she . . .'

I trail off. I can't explain, not now. I don't have the words.

Dad nods. 'All right, son. Don't you worry. We're going to deal with that Yan, aren't we? We're going to sort him out. Make sure he pays for what he's done.'

'Pay for what . . .' I say, frowning. I can't remember what he's done. Yan. Yan and Claire. The names float around my head. The two of them together make me angry. I try to separate them, but they refuse to be parted. It hits me with a sinking feeling. She is not mine. She will not always be there. She lied. She loves Yan, not me. She loves *him*. 'Claire loves Yan.'

'She's a stupid girl,' Dad says soothingly. 'You're better off without her. Just like I'm better off without your mum. Women are weak, Will. But he'll pay. He'll pay for all of it.'

'Yan will pay,' I say. It feels good.

'Yes, he will,' Dad says. 'And not just him. All of them. They're laughing at us. They're laughing, son. They take everything, and people like your mum don't see it. They think they're like injured animals. They want to look after them. But they're pests, Will. Like the grey squirrel driving out the red squirrel. They don't belong here and we have to fight for our land. Otherwise we'll be extinct and they'll have won.'

I bite my lip. I don't want them to win.

'We're all suckers for women, aren't we, son?' There's camaraderie in his voice. His eyes move down to my hands. 'I'm sorry. About this,' he says, gesturing to the tape. 'Patrick doesn't know you like I do. I knew you'd understand, if I could explain. You do understand, don't you, son?' He ruffles my hair.

My brain is working better, but I can't remember where this all started. Can't remember what I'm doing on my bed tied up. My chest hurts as though someone stamped on it.

Dad sighs heavily. 'I don't like arguing with you, son. I don't,' he says. 'But what you said before, about us planting evidence, it's not right. We can't let you go around saying those things, ruining everything. Do you see?'

Planting evidence. Yes. An image of Claire flashes into my mind. *You have to tell someone official. You have to say that in court.*

We have to save Yan.

'Save Yan. Yes. He didn't do it.'

'Yes, he did. You've got it wrong, son. No one's planted any evidence. We just need to tie up everything. Lock the boy away. He killed a man, son. He's a leech, just like his father.'

'He . . . He did? Are you sure?' I ask. My mind is buzzing. *Locked away. Away from Claire. He's a leech. This isn't his country. He's got no right stealing what's ours. What's mine.*

'You were there. You saw it, remember?' Dad says.

'You remember. You saw him with your own eyes. Saw him stick the knife in. Didn't you, son?'

My forehead is creasing in concentration. 'I saw . . . I saw . . .'

'You can teach the girl. Claire. You can bring her round. She likes you. I can see that now. I was wrong to stop you seeing her. Just trying to protect you, that's all. It's that Yan's fault. He's infecting her with his ideas. He's preying on her. You need to protect *her*, son. This is your chance to make things right.'

Make things right. No more Yan. Claire to myself.

'He was holding the knife,' I say tentatively.

'That's right. He was kneeling over Mr Best, wasn't he? Holding the knife. That's what you saw, isn't it?'

I nod.

England for the English. Foreigners Out.

'England for the English,' I say.

Dad looks surprised. He thinks for a moment, then he smiles. 'That's right. That,' he says, 'is the future. England for the English is what Patrick wants, what we all want, son. There's a new breed of politician. A party we can believe in. All of us. A party that sees the world like the rest of us do.'

'A party?' I ask.

'Patrick's party. Getting stronger every day, son. It's full of people like us, people who want what we want. They run the school you're going to go to. They'll see you right, son.'

I digest this. 'They'll look after me?'

'They'll make you stronger. Turn you into a man,

just like Patrick said. A leader. We need leaders, Will, people who aren't afraid to stand up for what's right. People who will reclaim our land,' Dad says. 'Reclaim our jobs, our taxes, our schools, our churches. Getting rid of the thieves who came here to take what's ours.'

'Thieves like Yan?' *Can you steal a person from someone? Yes. He stole Claire. He's stealing her right now. I can stop him.*

'Thieves like Yan.' Dad nods.

'This party. They want to get rid of them all?'

'Send them back home,' Dad corrects me. 'Send them back to where they came from.'

'And they can't come back?'

Dad shakes his head. 'Not if I have anything to do with it.'

'So Yan could be sent away? Not sent to prison?'

'Yan committed a crime. He's got to pay for that, son. You know that. His dad never paid,' Dad says looking down. 'He never paid for what he did. His son isn't going to get away with it like he did.'

'What did Yan's dad do?'

Dad looks down and swallows. 'He's responsible,' he says under his breath. 'He knows what he did.'

I feel my stomach clench. 'Mum?' I say.

An image. A memory. I had forgotten; now I remember. Dad, angry, pinning me down on the sofa. 'Has that man been here? Have you seen him in the house?'

I am scared. I don't know what to say.

'Son, I'm asking you. We're on the same side, me and you. You're my boy. You tell me the truth and everything's going to be OK. I just need to know. Has he been in the house?'

Mum is in the other room. They have been arguing, fighting – things have been smashed. I have been sitting on the sofa watching the television loudly. I look up at Dad. He lets go of me. He is calmer.

'Just tell me, Will. Just tell me the truth. You know we've always taught you to tell the truth.'

I take a deep breath. I nod.

'He was here? In the house? With your mother?'

I nod again.

'Thank you, son. Thank you.'

The image disappears. Dad closes his eyes for a moment, then he looks me right in the eye. 'That's right, son. That boy's father as good as killed your mum,' he says. 'He as good as took a knife and plunged it into her. You remember now, don't you?'

I search my mind; my head is starting to pound. *An image. Mum, in the water. I can see her. She is trying to stay afloat.*

'He killed Mum?'

I am sweating. I am hot, cold. There is a man there. She is drowning, going under. I can't help. I can't do anything. He is letting her die.

'Now do you want to see Yan pay? Now do you understand?' Dad asks.

I can't breathe. My chest is constricting. *Mum. Mum. No! No, please . . . It is too late. My mum has gone. She will never come back. Everything is over, everything is changed.*

'Son? Son, are you all right?'

Claire does not love me. She loves him. She lied. He has taken her from me.

They will pay. They will not take what isn't theirs any more. They will see that I am strong, that I am stronger than them. They will pay for what they have done. I nod. 'He'll pay,' I say. I am seething. I am full of red-hot fury. I will make them wish they'd never crossed me. I look down at my hands and Dad reddens.

'We'll get rid of this, shall we?' he asks, taking out some scissors and cutting the tape. 'Like I say, son, I was just trying to protect you. You understand, don't you? We're on the same side me and you. We'll always be on the same side, won't we?'

He looks at me expectantly, hopefully. I hold his gaze for a few seconds. Then I nod. I am not good. I am what I am. Douglas was right.

'The same side,' I say. I am strong. They will see. I will make them see. No one crosses me.

'Good for you, son. I knew you'd come round.'

He grins and I grin back. It feels good. We are in control. We are together.

'Father and son, changing things for the better. Sounds good, doesn't it?'

'Yes, it does,' I agree. I am not alone.

CHAPTER TWENTY

I go to school. My idea; Dad said I should stay at home. But I don't intend to hide. Why should I? I am who I am. I am proud of who I am. I can see clearly now. Douglas was right. Why fight my destiny?

Anyway, I want to see her. Want to have the satisfaction of telling Claire I know the truth. I want to look at her with my cold, angry eyes. I want her to know, want her to see. I will enjoy it. She thinks she has control over me but she doesn't. She is nothing to me any more.

When I get there, I see Claire standing at the school gate, waving. I walk past, ignoring her calls.

I walk down the corridor angrily, pushing people aside, not caring when they shout at me, when they turn round and threaten me. What are they going to do exactly? Nothing that worries me, that's for sure.

I go to the boys' toilets. Yan's brother is there. He's

looking at me hopefully. There's the hint of a smile on his face – tentative, friendly even.

He approaches me.

'Hodge, I . . . Claire talked to me. She said that . . .' His eyes cloud over as he talks. He isn't getting the reception he was hoping for. He clears his throat. 'Claire said that you . . . that this would stop. That you wanted it to.'

I stare at him. 'Nothing ever stops,' I snarl. I remember now. Pinning him against the wall, hitting him until he emptied his pockets. It's a memory. It's part of me. I am that person now. 'So give me your money.'

His eyes widen. 'But Claire said . . .'

'You shouldn't listen to girls,' I say. 'They lie. They're pathetic. You should remember that.'

We're nose to nose; I'm holding him by the scruff of the neck. He nods. He hands me his money. A crisp five-pound note. I take it.

'You're a loser,' I say. It makes me feel better.

I can see the terror in his eyes. Yan's brother is a parasite. He deserves this.

I let go of him and he slumps to the floor. I stay there, standing above him, for a few seconds. Just looking at him.

'You thought things were going to change,' I say. It isn't a question. He is too scared to answer anyway. 'Things don't change,' I say. 'Nothing ever changes. We are who we are. I'm who I am, and you're who you are. A snivelling wretch. A pathetic loser. You'll never fight back, and your brother's going to prison. That's it. So get used to it.'

I push open the door and walk through, letting it swing back with a bang. I enjoy the noise; I'm full of adrenaline. I want a punchbag, want to run somewhere – anything to let off the steam that's accumulating in my body. Is this how it always feels? Yes. It's a good feeling. It is a feeling of power, of omnipotence.

I stride down the hallway. I have History now. I'm going to enjoy myself. My teacher will learn not to disrespect me. I will make her wish she'd never picked on me.

I sit down at a desk near the back. The other desks begin to fill up and then Claire walks in and I feel my chest clench for a moment, then I breathe deeply and relax. She has betrayed me. I feel nothing for her.

She smiles at me and I look away. She looks con- fused, then hurt, then she shrugs and sits down.

I try to freeze. I feel nothing.

No, it's not true. I cannot ice over. I clench my fists but it's no use – I can't stop looking at her. Only when she's looking away, when she can't see, but my eyes won't leave her alone. My head is full of images of her laughing at me with Yan, holding his hand, telling him that I'll do exactly what she tells me to. The two of them together, walking away from me. Yan smiling the way his dad smiles at mine – the smile of a victor, the patronising smile of someone who's won.

They took Mum and now they have taken Claire.

But they haven't won yet. I do my best to steel myself.

The teacher walks in. She notices me, gives me a wry smile. A 'nice of you to join us' kind of smile. I look back stonily.

'I've marked your essays on the legacy of the Second World War,' she says. 'Those of you who submitted them.' She's looking at me again, with a raised eyebrow this time; I look away, bored. 'You made some interesting points, some of you,' she continues. 'Claire, I particularly liked your point about the huge changes that the war brought about but that change is rarely long lasting; as soon as another drama comes along everyone forgets and moves on to the next thing.'

I shoot a look at Claire, who is blushing slightly, like she always does when she receives praise.

'Of course nothing changes,' I say, more loudly than I'd intended. I was aiming for 'under the breath mutter' but I pretty much shout it.

The teacher looks at me quizzically. 'And why's that, Will?'

I fold my arms. Everyone's looking at me. I brazen it out. 'People are people,' I say.

'People are people? Will, insightful though that is, I'm not sure it's really an argument, is it?'

Her lips are moving upward at the edges; she's laughing at me. Like Claire. Like Yan. They're all laughing. But they won't laugh for long. They'll be laughing on the other side of their faces soon. I can feel the white anger descending. But now I'm in control; now I know what I'm doing. *This is who I am*, I repeat silently.

I stand up. 'You think the Second World War saw the last holocaust?' I ask, my voice icy. 'You think that people aren't killing each other, torturing each other, all over the world, all the time? You think that there aren't children being beaten, women mutilated, men killed, every single minute of every single day? That's life. That's humanity. That's who we are. You're either an abuser or a sufferer. You're strong or you're weak. No one learns anything from history; they just repeat it, over and over and over.'

The teacher is looking shocked; her mouth is open. Her eyes narrow, then she walks towards me.

'Just what are you trying to say, Will?'

'I'm saying that this is a waste of time,' I say levelly. 'Learning achieves nothing. We are achieving nothing sitting here.'

'You may be achieving nothing,' she says. 'Perhaps if you applied yourself –'

'Applied myself to learning about weak men who allowed others to brutalise them? What's the point?'

I stand up and head for the door; I turn back to see her looking at me, her mouth open in astonishment. I smile to myself. She knows I am right.

'There is no point,' I say. 'If I were you, I'd pack it in now.'

* * *

It's only when I reach the school gates that I realise Claire has been following me. She calls out my name; I turn round.

'Leaving lessons early? That's not like you.' I sound cold.

'Will? What's wrong with you? I thought yesterday . . . I thought you were OK. What's happened?'

She looks concerned. I remind myself that it's all an act. 'What's happened,' I say, 'is that I know what I'm doing. And I know what you're doing too.'

'What I'm doing?' She frowns. 'What do you mean? Will, you're not making any sense.'

'Yan,' I say. 'You're doing all of this for Yan, not me.'

'Doing what? Will, what are you going on about?'

'It's about him,' I round on her. 'It's all about Yan.'

'Of course it's about him. He's in prison, Will, for something he didn't do. But it's also about you. Tell me what happened since last night. You've changed. You're different.'

I shake my head in derision. 'I haven't changed,' I say. 'I'm just being true to myself.'

'Which self?' Her eyes are challenging; she's standing there, arms crossed, jaw firm.

'Look, just leave it, will you?' I grunt. 'Just go back to your boyfriend and leave me alone, OK?'

She blanches; I realise it's the truth. Even though I knew it before, it still hits me with a thud. 'You know about me and Yan?'

'I do now.'

'Is that what this is about?'

I swing round angrily. 'What this is about? No, Claire,' I say icily. 'No, this is not about you and Yan. This is about me, actually. Remember me? No, I didn't think so. I'm hardly important, am I, unless I can help your precious boyfriend. All that crap about believing in me – you just wanted me to save your boyfriend's arse.'

'No, that's not it. You're a good person, Will,' Claire says, her voice choking slightly. 'I just wanted you to see that.'

'You wanted me to testify against my own father,' I said.

'You have to,' Claire says tentatively. 'You still have to – you know that.'

'No, Claire, I don't have to.' I stare at her for a few seconds; she walks towards me.

'Yes, you do,' she says insistently. 'Will, don't run away from this. Yan needs you. You have to do the right thing. My parents spoke to the Police Commissioner this morning. He said if you go to the police station right away, he'll interview you himself. You have to go. You have to tell the truth.'

She's in my face, with that superior expression of hers, like she knows it all, like I'm just a child. My breathing quickens; I feel cornered, feel trapped, like she's bearing down on me. I want her out of my space. I push her. I don't think about it; I just have to get her away from me. She falls to the ground, protecting her face with her hands. She looks up at me, shocked, scared, as if she's seeing me for the first time. I'm backing away. Then I'm running, out of the school gates, down the road, towards the river. Always the river.

I reach a bench and sit down. I'm panting; my mind is racing. I can still see Claire looking up at me. She was scared of me. I pushed Claire. She said I'd never hurt her.

She was wrong.

Your life is not going to be easy, Will. You must prepare for that. Douglas said those words to me. But he was wrong. My life is going to be very easy. No one will cross me; no one will dare. I am powerful. I am strong. They are weak – all of them, even Claire. Especially Claire. She will not learn; I cannot help her.

I close my eyes. Images fill my head, clamouring for my attention; I give in to them.

Claire again, her eyes wide with fear. She is older, much older. She is begging me, she is pulling at my arm and imploring me, her voice high and agitated. 'You can't do this, Will. You can't get rid of them like this. They're British citizens, they belong here. This is wrong. This is so terribly wrong.'

I see it now. It is a new holocaust. I am the architect. They have brought it upon themselves; they had every opportunity to go. Now they will go on my terms. They are told the ships will take them home, but in truth they have no home – no one will take them. So the ship will take them to their deaths instead. Out in the ocean, out at sea, where no one has to see, no one has to take responsibility. The bodies will be disposed of in fires, bright flames that signal the future. England for the English. We will take our jobs back, our money, our houses, our land, our dignity.

'They are parasites and they don't belong here,' I say coldly. 'I must protect our people. I am saving us. Saving our country.'

'Then this isn't a country I want anything to do with. You put them on the ship and I go too.'

'You are English. You belong here.'

'No, Will, I don't. I belong with Yan, with my children. This isn't my country any more.'

I watch as she walks towards the ship, towards her end. She is looking back at me, her eyes full of hate.

I open my eyes. *I am who I am.* I can see it now. The others, like Claire, do not understand. They cannot; they need me to lead them, need me to act for them.

I stand up. I am ready now. I start to walk back home, at a brisk pace but not running this time.

When I get home, Dad is waiting for me. He looks unsettled.

'Son, what's going on?' he said. Patrick phoned to say the Chief Inspector's expecting you. He says he wants to talk to you. What about, son? Why does he want to see you? You remember what we agreed? You remember we're on the same side? Don't you? Don't you, son?' His eyes are wide, his voice quivering.

Everyone fears me. It is because I am strong and they can see that.

'You'll set things straight, won't you, son?'

I nod. Will the benefactor, Will the protector. 'Sure,' I say, watching his face relax with relief. 'Don't worry about it, Dad. Let's go.'

CHAPTER TWENTY-ONE

Dad drives me to the police station. He's wearing a suit. He's shaved. His hair has been combed awkwardly.

Claire and her parents are there too, waiting outside, for me. Claire's nose is grazed and one of her hands is bandaged. Her mother looks at me reproachfully. Claire's gaze is cold and unforgiving. It isn't her hand she's angry at me about, I know that, but I still can't take my eyes off it. I did that. Me.

That is who I am.

She walks towards me; Dad steps between us. 'You leave him alone, you hear?'

'It's OK, Dad,' I say. I look at her steadily.

She moves closer. 'Will, there's just one thing I don't understand.'

'You can't understand,' I say. 'You can't see the world as I see it. You never will.'

She shakes her head irritably. 'No, you don't understand,' she says. 'It's what you said about your dreams. Memories.'

I say nothing; I just raise an eyebrow.

'Rwanda,' she continues. 'You said you were there. But how could you have been? You said you'd been missing for fifty years. Since Auschwitz. You said that. So how could you have been in Rwanda? You couldn't have been. So it can't be a memory. It must be something else.'

I stay silent. 'The Rwandan genocide happened in 1994, Will. How could you have been there?' Her eyes are alight, with vindication, with determination. 'How?'

I open my mouth to tell her, to explain that I was watching from far away, that I was supposed to be there, but wouldn't go back. Couldn't go back. But I close it again. It was weakness that kept me away. I am not weak any more.

I look at her instead, my eyes hostile.

Eventually, to my relief, she turns back to her parents.

As she moves, I see that her eyes aren't as clear as I'd thought they were. She looks almost forlorn. She looks vulnerable.

Weak, I remind myself. There is only strong and weak, nothing in between.

Yan's dad bounds up the stairs suddenly. Dad freezes; his expression changes completely from apprehension to loathing. I narrow my eyes. Yan's dad doesn't notice, though. He runs up to me.

'You going to tell the truth? You going to help my son?' His face is gaunt, his eyes haunted. In them I see my mother, floating, her hair splayed out.

Silently I seethe at him. *Killer. You thought you were strong. But I am stronger. You will learn. You will regret crossing me.*

'You're going to tell them? That Yan didn't do it? Claire said you were there. You were always good friends, Will. You used to play football together, the two of you. Remember?'

He has taken hold of my shoulders. I look at his hands with distaste and move backwards so that they fall limply at his sides.

'Take your hands off him,' Dad says, the tone of his voice a warning in itself. 'You've done enough damage to this family.'

We walk towards the door, but something pulls me back. I am thrown to the ground and suddenly I am being hit, bitten, kicked. My hands move instinctively to protect my face. There is pain shooting through me. I can feel blood dripping from my nose. Confused, I throw my attacker off me. He returns, like an animal, he will not stop. I see his face; it is Yan's brother. He is kicking me, punching me. My eyes widen. He is no longer afraid of me.

'You think I am weak? You think my family is weak?' he shouts, his attack growing in strength. 'I am not weak. My brother is not weak. You're the bully, you're the weak one,' he shouts. His father pulls him off; as he is dragged away, still kicking, I see tears in his eyes.

Dad helps me to my feet. 'You all right, son? Little thug. Just like his brother.'

I look back and a policeman is restraining Yan's brother. I frown. I am shaking. It isn't fear. *We are who we are. People don't change.* And yet . . .

Dad is holding the door open. 'So you coming in?'

I look at him vaguely. 'I . . . I need the bathroom,' I say.

'Through there,' a policeman says, pointing to a door.

I walk in, stand over the basin, look at my reflection. *I am who I am. Accept it.*

The door opens and my father appears. 'You OK?' he asks.

I shake my head.

He walks towards me, puts a hand on my shoulder. 'Don't you let that little bastard get to you,' he says. 'You're a good boy, Will.'

I turn to look at him. It is as though he is suddenly several metres away. I cannot see him properly. *You're a good boy, Will.*

I pull away from him; I am sliding to the ground. My head is throbbing.

It's like a red-hot poker in the side of my head. I gasp in agony.

You're a good boy, Will. We're on the same side, me and you. The two of us, Will. We know what happened.

The words echo around my head. Dad's voice. A long time ago.

'Son? Son, what's wrong? If that boy has done anything to you . . . Wait there, I'm going to get someone. I'll be back in just a second . . .'

You tell me what you saw, Will.

People rush in. I am carried out of the bathroom.

No, son, no, you're getting confused. Now listen to me. He is insistent. He grabs me, too hard. I cry out. He lets go. 'Now don't make me hurt you,' he is saying, his voice full of emotion. 'I don't want to hurt you, Will. Just listen to me, will you? Let me tell you what happened . . .'

'A cell?' I hear Dad say.

'Only place with a bed. We'll call a doctor.'

I am placed on a blue plastic mattress. There is a hand on my hand. Dad's hand. He squeezes. 'You'll be OK, son. There's a doctor coming. Just close your eyes and rest.'

We are at the river. I see it in front of me. We are there, the three of us. Mum, Dad and me. It's early morning. Very early – so early the sun hasn't come up. I have not slept. I have been listening to them arguing, to thuds and crashes in the sitting room beneath me. I heard them leave the house and followed them. They are walking, and they are shouting. Mum starts crying. I move closer, take her hand. I can't bear to hear her cry.

239

She turns, shocked to see me. 'Will, go home, darling. You shouldn't be out here,' she says through her tears.

'I want to be with you,' I say.

'You sit here,' she says, pointing at a bench. 'Mum and Dad are having a grown-up talk. You sit here and you don't move. Promise?'

I nod and go to the bench. They aren't walking any more; they are standing still. I stare resolutely at the river.

Dad is shouting. He is using words I don't know, but I hear the anger in them, the accusations. 'You slut. You slept with him, I know you did.'

'No.' She grabs him, tries to keep him still, to make him look at her. 'No, Henry, I didn't. It's not like that.'

'Not like that? Then what's it like? He's been coming to the house. You've been seen together. Admit it. Tell the truth for once in your life, will you?'

'You don't understand. It's not like that. I –'

'You what? You WHAT?'

She's crying. 'You think I'm having an affair with him? You really think that? Jesus, can't you see? This isn't about you. This is about me. About the world around us. He's my friend. We're . . . We're . . .'

'You're what?' Dad thunders.

'You hate people. Hate everyone. You think people are the enemy, but they're not. That man, as you describe him, is a good man. He's created jobs. He's tried to be part of the community. But you and your

240

friends, the way you talk about him . . . He's been getting hate mail. Threats. You won't give him a chance, won't give anyone a chance. I can't be a part of that. I loved you. But I despise what you've become. I joined up. I joined the New Liberal party. I hate everything you believe in. I hate you.'

'You hate me?' He towers over her. I am scared. I edge backwards, behind the bench. I crouch down. I am watching them as though they are a scary television programme. 'You're leaving me for him? Is that what you're saying?'

'No. I don't want to leave. You're not listening. It's not like that. Nothing like that. I never . . . He came round to talk. About the movement. The New Liberal movement. Educating people, stopping the hatred, stopping the attacks . . .'

'You're lying!' He pushes her; she stumbles to the ground. She falls awkwardly on her ankle, topples, uses her hands to break her fall, but she rolls over, and then she is in the river.

Mum can't swim.

She is struggling, she is kicking.

I look at Dad. He doesn't move. She surfaces; she looks at him. I see her expression: bewilderment, betrayal, devastation, acceptance.

I run, suddenly, run out from behind the bench. I can't swim but I will save her.

But Dad sees me; he grabs me, holds me back. He is sobbing. His whole body is juddering.

'She can't swim,' I say. 'We have to get her out.'

'It's too late, she's already gone,' Dad says. 'She wanted it this way.'

I don't understand. 'Why?' I ask. 'Why?'

'Because she wasn't right,' Dad says. 'That's why she killed herself. You saw her jump into the river. She wanted to go. She didn't love us any more, you heard her say so. Not like me. I love you; I'm not going anywhere. We're on the same side, me and you. We're on the same side. The two of us, Will.' He leads me to the water's edge; she is floating, her hair splayed out. Her long, beautiful hair.

I open my eyes. I cannot move. I cannot speak.

I close them again. I am falling. I want to fall. I want to land, crashing on the floor, broken.

I never get what I want. I'm learning that, slowly, reluctantly.

I am watching over Rwanda. I hear a voice, shouting. It is my voice. I am shouting, 'No. No, don't do it.' I have seen too much pain. I cannot watch any more. It makes no difference that the boy is not me; he is there and that is enough. I watch the people in the school. I watch them suffer, watch mothers tending their sick children, hope evaporating as the hours tick by, as the truth becomes unavoidable, as they realise that there is no escape, no protection. 'No, no, you must not. You cannot.'

I am crying. I am helpless. I can do nothing.

Because I am not there.

Because I did not go back.

It hits me like a train.

Because I did not go back.

And I see that I must. I must go back. I must Return.

But I will be different. Everything will be different.

I will Return, and I will change. I will fight my destiny. I will not accept. I will never accept. I will fight . . . I will fight . . .

'Son?' Dad's looking at me worriedly. 'Where's the doctor?'

Another man is beside me. A light shines into my eyes; I close them on reflex, pull away.

'I'm fine.' I sit up.

The man peers at me. 'Does this sort of thing happen regularly?' he asks Dad.

'No, no. He's a healthy boy. That thug attacked him. If there's anything wrong with him, any lasting damage, I'll . . . I'll . . .'

'I'm fine.' I push him away, swing my legs over the side of the bed and climb down.

My head still feels as though it is being clamped in

a vice, but I don't care. I know. I remember. I remember everything.

'I want to get out of here.'

Dad nods. 'Are you sure you're OK, son? Where's the Police Commissioner? You don't have to do this now. You can do it whenever you want.'

'Now,' I say stonily. A policeman leads the way; I turn to look back at Dad. I find I can't. I follow the policeman to the Police Commissioner's office and he leaves the two of us alone. The door closes and I sit down. I make my statement slowly, precisely.

When I've finished, I go back to the foyer and Dad rushes over. 'All right, son? It went all right, did it?'

'Yes, Dad,' I say. 'I've got some things to do now. I'll see you later, OK?'

He nods; he can't do anything else.

I leave the police station and walk back towards the river.

CHAPTER TWENTY-TWO

It's strange how memories come back. Not like a dam opening, torrents of water tumbling through, but more like a small crack that allows a bit of water through, then a bit more, then gradually increases in size until there is nothing to hold back the flowing water from flooding downstream where it belongs.

He didn't try to save her.
He let her die.
He killed her.
Yan's dad wasn't there.
She didn't leave me.

My head drops down into my hands. My body is

moving, juddering; I realise I am crying. I cover my face with my hands.

I stay like that for a long time, until I am almost unable to move.

It is later. Minutes, hours; I don't know. I hear footsteps, then I feel an arm wrap round me; I open my eyes. It is Douglas.

'How do you always know where I am?'

He smiles. 'You're not that complicated,' he says.

'Yeah, well.' I shrug.

'You remember,' he says.

I nod. 'I remember.'

'Are you ready to accept your fate, Will? Are you ready to be who you are destined to be?'

I wipe my eyes and pull away from him.

Everything has changed.

'A Returner, you mean?'

He nods.

'Absorbing human misery? Remembering the sins of the world?' My voice sounds different; I don't recognise it.

Douglas hears it too; he nods again, but there's a flicker of something in his eyes. Uncertainty; wariness.

'Yes, Will,' he says.

'No,' I say. 'No, I'm not.'

He looks disappointed. 'I thought you understood, Will. I thought you saw that acceptance is the only way.'

'People don't change?' I say.

'People don't change,' he agrees.

'Except they do.'

I stand up, start walking. Douglas comes after me; he has to do a half-jog to keep up.

'You think I'm wrong? Will, change is impossible. Given the same choice in the same circumstance, we will always make the same decision. It's hard-wired into us.'

'No.' I stop suddenly and round on Douglas. 'No, you keep saying that but it isn't true. Dad changed. He loved Mum, he was a nice guy and he changed.'

'He simply allowed his true feelings to surface,' Douglas said.

'No.' I fold my arms. 'No.'

'Will, please. What you are doing can only hurt you. Fighting will only make things harder.'

'You know what my so-called destiny is?' I crouch down next to the river, pick up a stone and throw it in, disturbing some seagulls, who flap their wings irritably.

'We cannot know each other's destiny,' Douglas says.

'Yeah, well, let me tell you,' I say bitterly. 'There's going to be a holocaust. Worse than the Nazis.'

'Worse?'

'As bad. Does it matter? I'm going to kill people. Hundreds of thousands of them.'

Douglas looks at me sadly. 'You're scared?'

'Scared?' I grab his shoulders. 'Scared? No, I'm not

scared. I'm terrified. And not for me. For the world. For the people I'm meant to send to their deaths. Don't you see? I can't just passively sit back and become a monster. I won't do it. I'm not going to do it.'

'But –'

'But nothing.' I release Douglas. 'But nothing, Douglas. Everyone has a choice. Everyone. All the time. You can walk through a door or decide not to. You can let your past dictate your future, or you can throw two fingers up at it and walk away.'

'It's not that simple,' Douglas said. His eyes are cloudy, as though I've reminded him of something he doesn't want to think about.

'Yes, it is,' I said, firmly. 'You know, Claire pointed something out to me this morning. Rwanda. I remember Rwanda, Douglas.'

He frowns uncertainly. 'But you weren't . . .'

'Weren't there? No, I wasn't. I was meant to be. So how come I remember it?'

'I don't . . .'

'I'll tell you how,' I interrupt. 'I was watching from the wings. I wouldn't go back, see? After Auschwitz I refused to go back, refused to be a part of all the suffering. Said I couldn't do it any more. And so I watched what happened in Rwanda from wherever I was. Watched those people being mutilated, raped, knifed to death. Watched a boy trapping hundreds of people in a school to let them die. Watched all that brutality and all that doing nothing to stop it. And I realised that running away wasn't going to help anything because others would just step in. Running away achieves nothing. Claire was right. You have to stay and fight. That's why I came back. I came back to fight. And I'm going to, Douglas. I'm going to.'

'You came back to fight?' He looks shocked, uncertain. 'I don't understand. I –'

'And it's not just me, either.'

'It's not?'

'You have to choose too, Douglas. You have to choose to fight back.'

'Fight back?' Douglas frowned uncertainly. 'Will, that is not our role. That is not why we're here. That is not –'

'Yeah, I get it,' I interrupt rudely. 'You're here to suffer. But how about you change that? How about you take people like me on, pin them to the floor instead of letting them beat you up?'

'Pin you to the floor?' Douglas is shaking his head in bewilderment.

'And argue. Argue with me and people like my dad and the others who think that foreigners are to blame for all our problems, or people who believe different things, or people who eat different food or watch different television programmes. Tell them they're wrong. Make them see it. Force them to see it.'

Douglas's mouth is open, but he's not saying anything.

'Yan's dad didn't kill Mum,' I say. As I speak, I find myself blinking back tears. 'It wasn't his fault. It was

Dad's fault.' Douglas is still silent. I take a deep breath and continue. 'It's not Yan's fault that Claire likes him more than me. It's just the way it is. And Yan's brother . . .'

'His brother?' Douglas asks tentatively.

'The one I used to steal money from. The one who fought back. You should learn from him. All of you. If he can do it, you can too. You can change everything. And even if you can't change everything, you can change some things. Just some things can make a difference.'

'Will,' Douglas says, but I'm already walking away. My time is up; I've got to go.

The police car is parked right outside our house; everyone will have noticed. People are watching from behind curtains, pretending they need to walk down the street when really they're just trying to find out what's going on, to get a glimpse of whatever drama might be about to unfold.

Our front door opens; Dad is there, a policeman standing next to him. He's got the same expression on his face as Douglas had – bewilderment, confusion.

'Will? Will, son, where have you been? What's going on? The police are here. I can't get hold of Patrick. No one will tell me anything. Will?'

He's trying to sound gruff, confident, but I can see the doubt in his eyes. *It's me and you, son. We're a team.*

I walk towards him. I feel calm. Calm and purposeful. I wait for him to step aside, then walk into the house, into the sitting room. I sit down on the sofa, wait for him to sit down on his chair. Where he always sits.

He perches on it. He's leaning forward expectantly, drumming his fingers on his leg.

I take a deep breath, then I look at him, right at him, right into his eyes so that he really hears every word I say.

'He didn't do it, Dad.'

'What are you talking about? You mean that Yan? That filth? That . . .'

I hold my hand up. 'Stop,' I say. I feel very powerful suddenly. Like I felt when I was pummelling Douglas only different. Better. It feels more real. Less dangerous. More myself.

Dad looks at me warily. 'Don't you tell me to stop,' he says, but there is no conviction in his voice.

'Yan didn't kill Mr Best. Yan's dad didn't kill Mum. It wasn't them. And you know it.'

Dad opens his mouth; it stays like that for a few seconds but nothing comes out of it. 'I remember, Dad. I remember it all.'

He looks at me in confusion. Then his eyes fill with fear. 'No, son. No, you've got it wrong.'

'I remember. You killed her. You did it, Dad.'

'No!' He looks at me wide-eyed. 'He did it. He killed her. He filled her head with ideas. He made her unhappy with me. We were a team. We were the three musketeers. He was going to take her away from me.

Patrick warned me about him.' He puts his head in his hands. He is sobbing now. 'He –'

'Patrick is a liar. She didn't do anything, Dad. They were talking. They were only talking.'

He is disintegrating before my eyes. I feel pity for him.

'I'm not going to go along with Patrick's lies. Yan is someone's son, Dad. If we lie, if we persecute some-one for something they didn't do, we'll be on the wrong side of History. We'll be the enemy. We'll be the horror, Dad. Don't you see that?'

A policeman walks towards me. He handcuffs me.

'I'm arresting you, William Hodges, on suspicion of –'

'What?' Dad roars and pushes him to one side. 'What are you talking about? You can't arrest my son.'

'He can, Dad. I confessed to the murder. It was me, Dad. I did it.'

His eyes are wild now. 'No. No, son. You didn't. You –'

'I hid the knife at Yan's house,' I say. 'Under the floorboards. I did it. I was in a bad mood. That's what happened.'

'No, son.'

'Yes, Dad.'

He watches silently as the policeman leads me out of the house. Then he runs out towards the police car.

'It wasn't you. It was me,' he cries. 'Me and Patrick. We set it up. We did it. Take me. Take me.'

He is begging; his voice is hoarse.

The Police Commissioner gets out of the car, where he has been waiting all this time. His eyes flicker over to mine. My idea. His plan. I hadn't been sure Dad would admit the truth; I hadn't cared. Prison didn't frighten me. I'd seen it as a form of protection. For the others. For the people on the ships.

'You set it up?' he asks Dad. Dad looks at me again, looking for answers but there are none; he nods.

'Don't take my son,' he cries. 'He didn't have anything to do with it. It was me. Me and Patrick. We wanted the boy locked away, wanted people to think . . . They don't belong here. Leave my son . . .'

CHAPTER TWENTY-THREE

JULY 18TH 2016

There was this day, a few weeks ago. I was walking by the river, like I do sometimes, and maybe I was tired, or maybe I just felt like sitting down, I don't know – it doesn't matter. The point is, I sat down on one of those benches that have people's names on them, dead people, dead people who used to sit there before you did, maybe before you were even alive. I was just sitting there, hanging out. I wasn't doing anything in particular. Wasn't thinking about any-thing in particular. Watching the ducks, mostly, as far as I can remember. I saw a few people I know – Claire, Yan, walking along, maybe holding hands. I wasn't looking; it's nothing to do with me whether they were holding hands or not. I couldn't care in the slightest – but I pretty much ignored them like I usu-ally do. Other people are overrated in my opinion. Unlike ducks. I mean, how could a duck ever upset you? Ducks don't look at you like you're a total freak, or say stupid things, or ask you questions they know you don't want to answer. Ducks just hang out, like I was doing. They just get on with it.

The reason I'm telling you this is that, as far as I can remember, that day was the last time I felt happy. That is the last thing I can remember before everything changed.

But the thing about change is that it's unavoidable. The changes you dread, the ones you think are going to ruin your life, they're never all bad. You just have to look closely, just have to wait for the good bit to surface.

Dad's in prison now. Turns out Patrick's group, his political friends, they weren't just political. Turns out they were self-styled political terrorists. They thought a spate of murders up and down the country that could be blamed on foreigners would shake people out of their complacency, make them realise that the country was being taken over by foreigners, that they were sucking everything good out of our nation, that they had to be stopped. They set Yan up. He was just one of their victims. One of many, as it turned out. Half the group were involved in the criminal justice system, which made it easier for them to hide what they were doing. Dad was just one of their converts.

I could have been one too.

Maybe.

Probably.

I go and see him every day. He has good days and bad days – sometimes he thanks me, tells me I'm a good lad, promises he's going to be out soon. Other days he won't look at me, says I betrayed him, says I'm no kind of son, that he wishes I'd never been born. I don't mind. He's right both ways. To be honest, my feelings about him waver too.

Yan's free anyway. He's going to medical school apparently. Claire told me. She said she still wanted to be my friend, said she was really proud of me and that I could go and stay with her again if I wanted to, what with Dad in prison.

But I said no. Turns out as well that my mother has a sister I didn't know about. Mum and her fell out when Mum married Dad; they never spoke after the wedding. But she's going to move into our house while Dad's away. She looks a bit like Mum and she's got the same twinkle in her eye. So that's kind of a good thing, right?

Claire says I'm her project. She's got me reading up about politics. I'm thinking about joining the party that Mum joined. It feels good. And she knows when I'm losing it too – she knows how to snap me out of it when I feel myself beginning to freeze over.

I'm forcing myself to live in the present too, not allowing myself to let the ice descend. I recognise it now; anger, then ice, then chunks of time I can't account for. Chunks of time when I hurt people, unencumbered by conscience, by morality, by . . . me.

And Douglas is trying too. All of them are. Trying to fight back, even just in little ways.

I have normal dreams now. Ones that involve flying and turning up for exams without any clothes on. Ones that aren't about death and suffering and torture. I still have one of the old dreams. The one about the future. But it changes now. Sometimes it's the same as it was before, but sometimes I'm on the other side, stopping the ship from sailing off. And sometimes there is no ship, sometimes the world is different and people don't hate each other after all. Claire says that's because the future isn't set, because there is no destiny, just the life you carve out for yourself. She says I can carve out any life I choose. I like it when she says that.

And so I sit and watch the ducks. I'm on my own again, but I'm not lonely, not any more. And as I sit here, I realise that maybe I will be happy again. I don't know what's going to happen in the future, but I do know that it's open. I know that it isn't set in stone. Nothing is. Not if you don't want it to be.

In fact, I think to myself, maybe, just maybe, I'm a little bit happy right now.

Also by Gemma Malley from Bloomsbury

The Declaration

'One of the best written
books of the year'
Sunday Telegraph.

Gemma Malley

Turn the page to read an extract.

Chapter One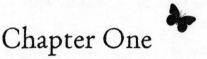

11 January, 2140

My name is Anna.

My name is Anna and I shouldn't be here. I shouldn't exist.

But I do.

It's not my fault I'm here. I didn't ask to be born. But that doesn't make it any better that I was. They caught me early, though, which bodes well. That's what Mrs Pincent says, anyway. She's the lady that runs Grange Hall. We call her House Matron. Grange Hall is where I live. Where people like me are brought up to be Useful – the 'best of a bad situation', Mrs Pincent says.

I don't have another name. Not like Mrs Pincent does. Mrs Pincent's name is Margaret Pincent. Some people call her Margaret, most people call her Mrs

Pincent, and we call her House Matron. Lately I've started to call her Mrs Pincent too, although not to her face – I'm not stupid.

Legal people generally have at least two names, sometimes more.

Not me, though. I'm just Anna. People like me don't need more than one name, Mrs Pincent says. One is quite enough.

Actually, she doesn't even like the name Anna – she told me she tried to change it when I first came here. But I was an obstinate child, she says, and I wouldn't answer to anything else, so in the end she gave up. I'm pleased – I like the name Anna, even though my parents gave me that name.

I hate my parents. They broke the Declaration and didn't care about anyone else but themselves. They're in prison now. I don't know where. None of us knows anything about our parents any more. Which is fine by me – I'd have nothing to say to them anyway.

None of the girls or boys here has more than one name. That's one of the things that makes us different, Mrs Pincent says. Not the most important thing, of course – having one name is really just a detail. But sometimes it doesn't feel like a detail. Sometimes I long for a second name, even a horrible one – I wouldn't care what it was. One time I even asked Mrs Pincent if I could be Anna Pincent, to have her name after mine. But that made her really angry and she hit me hard across the head and took me off hot meals for a whole week. Mrs Larson, our Sewing Instructor, explained later that it had been an insult to suggest that someone like me could have Mrs Pincent's name. As if she could be related to me.

Actually I do sort of have another name, but it's a pre-name, not an after-name. And everyone here has got the same one, so it doesn't really feel like a name. On the list that Mrs Pincent carries around with her, I'm down as:

Surplus Anna.

But really, it's more of a description than a name. We're all Surpluses at Grange Hall. Surplus to requirements. Surplus to capacity.

I'm very lucky to be here, actually. I've got a chance to redeem my Parents' Sins, if I work hard enough and become employable. Not everyone gets that kind of chance, Mrs Pincent says. In some countries Surpluses are killed, put down like animals.

They'd never do that here, of course. In England they help Surpluses be Useful to other people, so it isn't quite so bad we were born. Here they set up Grange Hall because of the staffing requirements of Legal people, and that's why we have to work so hard – to show our gratitude.

But you can't have Surplus Halls all over the world for every Surplus that's born. It's like straws on a camel's back, Mrs Pincent says. Each and every Surplus could be the final straw that breaks the camel's back. Probably, being put down is the best thing for everyone – who would want to be the straw that broke the back of Mother Nature? That's why I hate my parents. It's their fault I'm here. They didn't think about anyone except themselves.

I sometimes wonder about the children who are put down. I wonder how the Authorities do it and whether it hurts. And I wonder what they do for maids and housekeepers in those countries. Or handymen. My friend Sheila says that they do sometimes put children down here too. But I don't believe her. Mrs Pincent says Sheila's imagination is far too active and that it's going to be her downfall. I don't know if her imagination is too active, but I do think she makes things up, like when she arrived and she swore to me that her parents hadn't signed the Declaration, that she was Legal and that it had been a big mistake because her parents had Opted Out of Longevity. She insisted over and over again that they'd be coming to collect her once they'd sorted it all out.

They never did, of course.

There're five hundred of us here at Grange Hall. I'm one of the eldest and I've been here the longest too.

I've lived here since I was two and a half – that's how old I was when they found me. I was being kept in an attic – can you believe that? The neighbours heard me crying, apparently. They knew there weren't meant to be any children in the house and called the Authorities. I owe those neighbours a great deal, Mrs Pincent says. Children have a way of knowing the truth, she says, and I was probably crying because I wanted to be found. What else was I going to do – spend my life in an attic?

I can't remember anything about the attic or my parents. I used to, I think – but I'm not really sure. It could have been dreams I was remembering. Why would anyone break the Declaration and have a baby just to keep it in an attic? It's just plain stupid.

I can't remember much about arriving at Grange Hall either, but that's hardly surprising – I mean, who remembers being two and a half? I remember feeling cold, remember screaming out for my parents until my throat was hoarse because back then I didn't realise how selfish and stupid they were. I also remember getting into trouble no matter what I did. But that's all, really.

I don't get into trouble any more. I've learnt about responsibility, Mrs Pincent says, and am set to be a Valuable Asset.

Valuable Asset Anna. I like that a lot more than Surplus.

The reason I'm set to be a Valuable Asset is that I'm a fast learner. I can cook fifty dishes to top standard, and another forty to satisfactory. I'm not as good with fish as I am with meat. But I'm a good seamstress and am going to make someone a very solid housekeeper according to my last appraisal. If my attention to detail improves, I'll get an even better report next time. Which means that in six months, when I leave Grange Hall, I might go to one of the better houses. In six months it's my fifteenth birthday. It'll be time to fend for myself then, Mrs Pincent says. I'm lucky to have had such good training because I Know My Place, and people in the nicest houses like that.

I don't know how I feel about leaving Grange Hall. Excited, I think, but scared too. The furthest I've ever been is to a house in the village, where I did an internship for three weeks when the owner's own housekeeper was ill. Mrs Kean, the Cooking Instructor, walked me down there one Friday night and then she brought me back when it was over. Both times it was dark so I didn't see much of the village at all.

The house I was working in was beautiful, though. It was nothing like Grange Hall – the rooms were painted in bright, warm colours, with thick carpet on the floor that you could kneel on without it killing your knees, and huge big sofas that made you want to curl up and sleep for ever.

It had a big garden that you could see out of all the windows, and it was filled with beautiful flowers. At the back of the garden was something called an Allotment where Mrs Sharpe grew vegetables sometimes, although there weren't any growing when I was there. She said that flowers were an Indulgence and frowned upon by the Authorities. Now that food couldn't be flown around the world, everyone had to grow their own. She said she thought that flowers were important too, but that the Authorities didn't agree. I think she's right – I think flowers can be just as important as food, sometimes. I think it depends what you're hungry for.

In the house, Mrs Sharpe had her radiators on sometimes, so it was never cold. And she was the nicest, kindest woman – once when I was cleaning her bedroom she offered to let me try on some lipstick. I said no, because I thought she might tell Mrs Pincent, but I regretted it later. Mrs Sharpe talked to me almost like I wasn't a Surplus. She said it was nice to have a young face about the place again.

I loved working there – mainly because of Mrs Sharpe being so nice, but also because I loved looking at the photos she had all over her walls of incredible-looking places. In each photo, there was Mrs Sharpe, smiling, holding a drink or standing in front of a beautiful building or monument. She said that the photographs were mementos of each of her holidays. She went on an international holiday three times a year at least, she told me. She said that she used to go by aeroplane but now energy tariffs meant that she had to go by boat or train instead, but she still went because you have to see the world, otherwise what's the point? I wanted to ask 'The point of what?' but I didn't because you're not meant to ask questions, it's not polite. She said she'd been to a hundred and fifty different countries, some more than twice, and I tried to stop my mouth dropping open because I didn't want her to know that I hadn't even known there were that many countries in the world. We don't learn about countries at Grange Hall.

Mrs Sharpe has probably been to four hundred and fifty-three countries now, because it was a whole a year ago that I was at her house. I wish I were still her housekeeper. She didn't hit me even once.

It must be amazing to travel to foreign countries. Mrs Sharpe showed me a map of the world and showed me where England is. She told me about the deserts in the Middle East, about the mountains in India and about the sea. I think my favourite place would be the desert because apparently there are no people there at all. It would be hard to be Surplus in the desert – even if you knew you were one really, there wouldn't be anyone else around to remind you.

I'll probably never see any desert, though. Mrs Pincent says it's all disappearing fast because they can build on it now. Desert is a luxury this world can't afford, she says. And I should be worrying about the state of my ironing, not thinking of places I'll never be able to go to. I'm not sure she's exactly right about that, although I'd never say that to her. Mrs Sharpe said she had a housekeeper once who used to go with her travelling around the world, doing her packing and organising tickets and things like that. She had her for forty years, she told me, and she was very sad to see her go because her new housekeeper can't take the hot temperatures, so she has to leave her behind when she goes away. If I could get a job with a lady who travels a lot, I don't think I'd mind the hot temperatures. The desert's the hottest place of all and I'm sure I'd love it there.

'Anna! Anna, will you come here this minute!'

Anna looked up from the small journal Mrs Sharpe had given her as a parting gift and quickly returned it, and her pen, to its hiding place.

'Yes, House Matron,' she called hurriedly, and rushed out of Female Bathroom 2 and down the corridor, her face flushed. How long had Mrs Pincent been calling her? How had she not heard her call?

The truth was that she'd never realised how absorbing it could be to write. She'd had Mrs Sharpe's journal for a year now. It was a small, fat book covered in pale pink suede and filled with thick, creamy pages that looked so beautiful she couldn't ever imagine ruining them by making a single mark on that lovely paper. Every so often she'd taken it out to look at it. She would turn it over in her hands, guiltily enjoying the soft texture of the suede against her skin before secreting it away again. But she'd never written in it – not until today, that is. Today, for some reason, she had taken it out, picked up a pen, and without even thinking had started to write. And once she'd started, she found she didn't want to stop. Thoughts and feelings that usually lay hidden beneath worries and exhaustion suddenly came flooding to the surface as if gasping for air.

Which was all very well, but if it was discovered, she would be beaten. Number one, she wasn't allowed to accept gifts from anyone. And number two, journals and writing were forbidden at Grange Hall. Surpluses were not there to read and write; they were there to learn and work, Mrs Pincent told them regularly. She said that things would be much easier if they didn't have to teach them to read and write in the first place, because reading and writing were a dangerous business; they made you think, and Surpluses who thought too much were useless and difficult. But people wanted maids and housekeepers who were literate, so Mrs Pincent didn't have a choice.

If she were truly Valuable Asset material, she would get rid of the journal completely, Anna knew that. Temptation was a test, Mrs Pincent often said. She'd already failed it twice – first by accepting the gift and now by writing in it. A true Valuable Asset wouldn't succumb to temptation like that, would they? A Valuable Asset simply wouldn't break the rules.

But Anna, who never broke any rules, who believed that regulations existed to be followed to the letter, had finally found a temptation that she could not resist. Now that the journal bore her writing, she knew that the stakes had been raised, and yet she could not bear to lose it, whatever the cost.

She would simply have to ensure it was never found, she resolved as she raced towards Mrs Pincent's office. If no one knew her guilty secret, then perhaps she could bury her feelings along with the journal and convince herself that she wasn't evil after all, that the little fragment of peace she had carved out for herself at Grange Hall was not really in jeopardy.

Before she turned the corner, Anna took a quick look at herself and smoothed down her overalls. Surpluses had to look neat and orderly at all times, and the last thing Anna wanted was to irk Mrs Pincent unnecessarily. She was a Prefect now, which meant she got second helpings at supper when there was food left over, and an extra blanket that meant the difference between a good night's sleep and one spent shivering from the cold. No, the last thing she wanted was any trouble.

Taking a deep breath, and focusing herself so that she would appear to Mrs Pincent the usual calm and organised Anna, she turned the corner and knocked on the House Matron's open door.

Also by Gemma Malley from Bloomsbury

The Resistance

From the bestselling author of *The Declaration*

Gemma Malley

The sequel to *The Declaration*

Turn the page to read an extract.

Peter followed his grandfather down the corridor in silence, trying to ignore his heart thudding loudly in his chest. They took the lift up to the third floor, which was empty but for patrolling guards, luxurious but for the heavy locks on heavy-looking doors.

'And this is my office,' his grandfather said, eventually, keying in a code which opened a large door. 'Changes every day, this code,' his grandfather said, noticing Peter's staring eyes. 'Best security system in the whole world.'

Peter nodded silently, and only just stopped himself from gasping as he looked around. The room was opulent in a way that Peter had never seen before: polished floorboards covered with heavy rugs, ceilings high enough for three men to stand on each other's shoulders, lights everywhere – embedded in the ceiling, standard lamps, side lights, lights in cupboards, lights on the floor. It was warm, too – a fire crackled under a huge mantelpiece and he immediately imagined Anna curled up comfortably in front of it, reading. She'd love it, he thought to himself bitterly.

But the thing that drew Peter's eyes, the thing that made this room bigger, better, more incredible than any other room he'd been in, was the view – of the river, of London. The window behind his grandfather's desk was enormous and – incredibly – it could be opened, something his grandfather appeared to take great delight in demonstrating.

'We do things differently here, Peter,' he said, his eyes glinting. 'The rules that apply to others don't apply to us.'

Peter cleared his throat, trying his best to appear relaxed and confident, but underneath the facade, he was filled with a sense of dread – dread that he was going to be expelled from Pincent Pharma before he'd been of any use to the Underground, dread that he'd allowed his heart to rule his head, stupidly, foolishly.

'So, Peter,' his grandfather said, sitting down at his large, mahogany desk and motioning for Peter to take the chair on the other side of it. 'How are you getting on?'

Peter looked at him cautiously and forced a smile. 'Fine. I'm getting on fine.'

Richard Pincent nodded. 'Fine. I see.' He sat back in his chair. Peter's eyes had been darting about the room curiously, and he made himself look down instead. Anna had told him before that his eyes were dangerous – they unsettled people, they refused to compromise. 'But you've decided not to sign the Declaration.'

Peter bit his lip. 'Actually,' he said, his throat

feeling suddenly dry, 'I haven't really decided. I'm . . . thinking about it.' Inside, he knew he was doing the right thing; he still felt slightly sick even suggesting he might sign.

'Peter, I wonder if you'd let me tell you the story of Longevity.'

Peter looked up briefly. 'I know the story,' he said, before he could stop himself. 'I saw the film.'

His grandfather held his gaze for a few seconds. 'Indulge me, Peter, just for a few minutes?'

Peter nodded quickly, kicking himself.

'The story of Longevity,' his grandfather said, standing up and walking towards the vast window behind him, 'starts many thousands of years ago, when humans first walked this earth.'

Peter found his eyes drawn back to the window and its spectacular view. Slowly, he scanned the horizon, taking in the buildings on the other side of the river, the river itself. Somewhere out there were his friends; somewhere out there were the other members of the Underground, his comrades. They were outside and they were depending on him, just like Anna had in Grange Hall. And just like then, he wasn't going to let anyone down.

'As soon as man worked out how to communicate, how to develop tools, the fight against death had begun. Man learnt how to protect himself from predators, to insulate himself against his environment. Through discovery, he extended his lifespan. But that wasn't enough, Peter.'

3

Peter nodded seriously. 'It wasn't?'

'No. Because man still feared death; feared disappearing into nothingness, feared how death made each life insignificant. And so he sought to attack the things that ended his life – disease and illness. Longevity did not appear out of nowhere, Peter; it is simply the latest invention in a long line of inventions – antibiotics, vaccinations, X-rays, even sanitation – all of which extended man's life substantially. If you reject Longevity, then why not reject all of medicine? If nature's way is the best way, then surely a bandage, antiseptic, any intervention at all in fact, is morally wrong, is "unnatural".'

Peter felt his cheeks redden. 'I haven't . . . I mean, I haven't rejected Longevity. I just haven't decided.'

His grandfather looked at him impatiently. 'Then decide, Peter,' he said, a hint of menace in his voice. 'Decide. Choose life, Peter. Man has always searched for eternal life – through religion, through philosophy. And you are being offered it on a platter.'

'Religion?' Peter frowned.

'You won't know much about religion, Peter; people have no need of it now,' he said. 'But people used to put great store by the notion of a god, or gods. Great men spent many hours debating the subtle nuances of different religions, arguing that belief in a higher being, in an afterlife, in redemption, placed humans above animals; that it made them special, superior. Great wars were fought between countries that held different religious beliefs, even when the

4

points of contention were so small as to be laughable now. But religions were based on the pretext that humans were fallible, that humans died. Only gods lived for ever; only through religion could humans hope to achieve salvation and some sort of existence after death. Now, we ourselves live for ever. Now, Peter, we are our own gods. Through Longevity, we are more powerful than anything man has ever imagined.'

Peter cleared his throat. 'I heard,' he said carefully, 'that religion was suppressed by the Authorities because its leaders didn't agree with Longevity.'

His grandfather's eyes clouded over and Peter kicked himself for speaking his mind yet again. 'It's true enough that religious leaders condemned Longevity,' his grandfather said darkly. 'But why do you think that was, Peter? I'll tell you why. It was because they were desperate to hold on to power and influence. Do you think people miss being told what to do, being encouraged to mistrust others because they happened to believe in a different god? Do you think people miss the corruption, the genocide, the wars, the terrorist attacks that were all implemented in the name of some god or other? Do you think they are sorry to be free of all of this? To make their own decisions?'

Peter said nothing, and his grandfather smiled triumphantly. 'Of course,' he said lightly, 'personally, I'm rather grateful to religion. You see, we used to be rather behind the US when it came to scientific research; everyone expected their scientists to come up with something like Longevity, not us. But their religious leaders banned research on stem cells. Banned it – can you believe that? So their research dried up. We took the baton, and . . . well, you know the rest.'

Peter frowned. He felt confused, didn't know what to say. 'There used to be young people,' he said eventually. 'Now there aren't any.'

His grandfather nodded. 'That's what people have chosen, Peter. There are difficult choices to be made and that was one that was unavoidable. But is it really such a bad thing?' He shook his head dismissively. 'These young people you talk of, they had nothing. No hope, no prospects. They were turning to crime to support themselves, Peter. They terrorised communities.'

He walked back to his desk, leaning against the front of it so that he was just inches away from Peter. 'And then we discovered Longevity. The Holy Grail, Peter. The secret to eternal life.'

Peter took a deep breath. 'And nature?'

'Nature?' His grandfather shook his head with disgust. 'Nature is our enemy, Peter. She has always been our enemy. Nature held sway over humankind, striking us down at will, ravaging our bodies with cancer, killing women during childbirth, creating plagues that wiped out entire cities. All these are the gifts of nature, Peter. She is no friend of humans.'

'And Longevity is?' Peter asked uncertainly.

'Yes, it is. Longevity was created to save us, Peter,' his grandfather said gravely. 'Imagine if Anna was dying. Wouldn't you want to give her Longevity then? Wouldn't you want to save her life? Yes or no?'

Peter didn't say anything for a second or two. 'I . . . I don't know,' he said. He realised as he spoke that he was telling the truth. Then he shook himself. It was a trick question. Wanting to save someone's life didn't make Longevity OK.

'No,' his grandfather smiled. 'I don't suppose you do. The truth of the matter is that nothing is black and white – it is all shades of grey. You might want to think about that before you throw your life away for a lost cause.'

As soon as Peter had left, Richard picked up the phone and dialled Adrian's private line.

'Adrian,' he said, when the phone was answered. 'Where are we at with the research grants?'

'Grants?'

Richard frowned. It was a woman's voice.

'I'm sorry. I thought this was Adrian Barnet's line.'

'It was. Now it's my line. My name is Hillary Wright. I'm the new Deputy Secretary General.'

Richard took a few seconds to digest this information. 'And Adrian?'

'Adrian has been redeployed.'

Richard nodded. 'Then welcome to your post,' he said jovially. 'This is Richard Pincent speaking. Of Pincent Pharma.'

Also by Gemma Malley from Bloomsbury

Look out for:

The Revelation

Coming soon

The exciting conclusion to *The Declaration* trilogy